NOAH
BARLEYWATER
RUNS
AWAY

Also by John Boyne

NOAH BARLEYWATER RUNS AWAY

A fairytale by

John Boyne

Illustrated by Oliver Jeffers

David Fickling Books

OXFORD · NEW YORK

NOAH BARLEYWATER RUNS AWAY
A DAVID FICKLING BOOK 978 0 385 61895 3

Published in Great Britain by David Fickling Books,
a division of Random House Children's Books
A Random House Group Company

This edition published 2010

1 3 5 7 9 10 8 6 4 2

Text copyright © John Boyne, 2010
Illustrations © Oliver Jeffers, 2010

The right of John Boyne and Oliver Jeffers to be identified as
the author and illustrator of this work has been asserted in accordance
with the Copyright, Designs and Patents Act 1988.

The Random House Group Limited supports the Forest Stewardship Council (FSC),
the leading international forest certification organization.
All our titles that are printed on Greenpeace-approved FSC-certified paper
carry the FSC logo. Our paper procurement policy can be found at
www.rbooks.co.uk/environment.

Mixed Sources
Product group from well-managed
forests and other controlled sources
www.fsc.org Cert no. TT-COC-2139
© 1996 Forest Stewardship Council
FSC

Set in New Baskerville

DAVID FICKLING BOOKS
31 Beaumont Street, Oxford, OX1 2NP

www.kidsatrandomhouse.co.uk
www.rbooks.co.uk

Addresses for companies within The Random House Group Limited can be found at:
www.randomhouse.co.uk/offices.htm

THE RANDOM HOUSE GROUP Limited Reg. No. 954009

A CIP catalogue record for this book is available from the British Library.

Printed and bound in Great Britain by Clays Ltd, St Ives plc.

For Katie Lynch

Chapter One

The First Village

Noah Barleywater left home in the early morning, before the sun rose, before the dogs woke, before the dew stopped falling on the fields.

He climbed out of bed and shuffled into the clothes he'd laid out the night before, holding his breath as he crept quietly downstairs. Three of the steps had a loud creak in them where the wood didn't knit together correctly so he walked very softly on each one, desperate to make as little noise as possible.

In the hallway he took his coat off the hook but didn't put his shoes on until he had already left the house. He walked down the laneway, opened the gate, went through and closed it again, treading as lightly as he could in case his parents heard the sound of the gravel crunching beneath his feet and came downstairs to investigate.

It was still dark at this hour and Noah had to squint to make out the road that twisted and turned up ahead. The growing light would allow him to sense

1

any danger that might be lurking in the shadows. When he got to the end of the first quarter-mile, at just that point where he could turn round one last time and still make out his home in the distance, he stared at the smoke rising from the chimney that stretched upwards from the kitchen fireplace and thought of his family inside, all safely tucked up in their beds, unaware that he was leaving them for ever. And despite himself, he felt a little sad.

Am I doing the right thing? he wondered, a great blanket of happy memories trying to break through and smother the fresher, sadder ones.

But he had no choice. He couldn't bear to stay any longer. No one could blame him for that, surely. Anyway, it was probably best that he went out to make his own way in the world. After all, he was already eight years old and the truth was, he hadn't really done anything with his life so far.

A boy in his class, Charlie Charlton, had appeared in the local newspaper when he was only seven, because the Queen had come to open a day centre for all the grannies and grandads in the village, and he had been chosen to hand her a bunch of flowers and say, *We're SO delighted you could make the journey, ma'am.* A photograph had been taken where Charlie was grinning like the Cheshire cat as he presented the bouquet, and the Queen wore an expression that suggested she had smelled something funny but was far too well-brought-up to comment on it; he'd seen that expression on the Queen's face before and it always made him giggle. The photo had been placed on the school notice board the following day and had remained there until someone – *not* Noah – had drawn a moustache on Her Majesty's face and written some rude words in a speech bubble coming out of her mouth that nearly gave the headmaster, Mr Tushingham, a stroke.

The whole thing had caused a terrible scandal, but at least Charlie Charlton had got his face in the papers and been the toast of the schoolyard for a few days. What had Noah ever done with his life to compare with that? Nothing. Why, only a few days before he'd tried to make a list of all his achievements, and this is what he'd come up with:

> *1. I have read fourteen books from cover to cover.*
> *2. I won the bronze medal in the 500 metres at Sports Day last year and would have won silver if Breiffni O'Neill hadn't jumped the gun and got a head start.*
> *3. I know the capital of Portugal. (It's Lisbon.)*
> *4. I may be small for my age but I'm the seventh cleverest boy in my class.*
> *5. I am an excellent speller.*

Five achievements at eight years of age, he thought at the time, shaking his head and pressing the tip of his pencil to his tongue even though his teacher,

Miss Bright, screamed whenever anyone did that and said they would get lead poisoning. *That's one achievement for every* . . . He thought about it and did a series of quick calculations on a bit of scrap paper. *One achievement for every one year, seven months and six days. Not very impressive at all.*

He tried to tell himself that this was the reason he was leaving home, because it seemed a lot more adventurous than the real reason, which was something he didn't want to think about. Not this early in the morning, anyway.

And so here he was, out on his own, a young soldier on his way to battle. He turned round, thinking to himself, *That's it! I'll never see that house again now!* and continued on his way, strolling along with the air of a man who knows that, come the next election, there's every chance he will be elected mayor. It was important to look confident – he realized that very early on. After all, there was a terrible tendency among adults to look at children travelling alone as if they were planning a crime of some sort. None of them ever thought that it might just be a young chap on his way to see the world and have a great adventure. They were so small-minded, grown-ups. That was one of their many problems.

I must always be looking ahead as if I'm expecting to see someone I know, he told himself. *Behave like a person with a destination in mind, then there's less chance of my being stopped or asked my business. When I see people,* he thought, *I'll pick up the pace a little, as if I'm in a terrible hurry and am sure to be beaten black and blue if I don't get where I'm going when I'm supposed to be there.*

It wasn't long before he reached the first village, and by the time he got there he was starting to feel a little hungry as he hadn't had anything to eat since the night before. The smell of eggs and bacon spilled out from the open windows of the houses that ran up and down the streets. He licked his lips and looked at the windowsills. In the books he had read, grown-ups often left pies and cakes there with steam rising out of their peaked pastry hats, just so ravenous boys like him could come along and steal them away. But no one seemed to be that stupid in the first village. Or maybe they just hadn't read the same books as he had.

But then, a stroke of good luck! An apple tree appeared before him. It hadn't been there a moment before – at least he hadn't noticed it – but here it was now, standing tall and proud in the early morning breeze, its branches weighed down with shiny green apples. He pulled up short and grinned, delighted by his discovery, because he loved apples so much, his mother always said that one day, if he wasn't careful, he would turn into an apple. (And that would *definitely* get his name in the papers.)

Breakfast! he thought, running forward, but as he did so, one of the branches of the tree – the one that had been leaning most towards him – seemed to rise up a little and press itself closer to the trunk, as if somehow it knew that he'd been planning on stealing one of its treasures.

'How extraordinary!' said Noah, hesitating for a moment before stepping forward again.

This time the tree made a great grunting sound – a similar noise to the one his father always made when he was reading the newspaper and Noah kept bothering him to come outside and play football – and if he hadn't known any better, he could have sworn that the tree was edging its way to the left, moving away from him, its branches pressing even tighter to the trunk now, its apples trembling a little in fright.

'But it can't be,' he decided, shaking his head. 'Trees don't move. And apples *certainly* don't tremble.'

And yet it *was* moving. It was most certainly moving. It even seemed to be speaking to him. But what was it saying? A quiet voice whispering beneath the bark . . . *'No, no, please, no, don't, I beg of you, no, no . . .'*

Well, that's enough nonsense for this time of the morning, Noah decided, throwing himself against the tree, which immediately froze as he wrapped his arms around it and plucked three apples – one, two, three – off the branches before jumping away again, popping one in his left-hand pocket, one in his right, and taking a great bite out of the third in triumph.

The tree wasn't moving at all now; if anything, it seemed to be drooping a little.

'Well, I was hungry!' he cried aloud, as if he had to explain himself to the tree. 'What was I to do?'

The tree didn't respond, and Noah shrugged his shoulders and walked away, feeling a little guilty as he did so but shaking his head quickly as if he could throw those emotions out of his ears and leave them behind, bouncing up and down on the pebbled streets of the first village.

But just at that moment a voice called out from behind him – 'Hey, you!' – and he turned to see a man marching quickly in his direction. 'I saw you!' the man cried, stabbing a gnarly finger in the air over and over. 'What do you think you're doing, eh?'

Noah froze for a moment, then turned on his heel and started running. He couldn't be caught this quickly. He couldn't allow himself to be sent back. And so, without a moment's hesitation, he ran away from the man as fast as he could, leaving behind him a trail of dust that gathered up into a dark cloud and rained down on the first village for the rest of the morning, covering the gardens and freshly bedded spring plants, making the villagers cough and splutter for hours on end – a trail of destruction for which Noah didn't even realize he was responsible.

In fact, it wasn't until he was sure he was no longer being chased that he slowed down, and this

Fig 1

TWO APPLES,
One with a BITE taken out.

was when he realized that the apple in his left-hand pocket had fallen out while he was running.

Never mind, he thought, *I still have the one in my right.*

But no, that was gone too, and he hadn't even heard it fall.

Annoying! he thought. *But at least I have the one in my hand—*

But no, somewhere along the way that had vanished too, and he hadn't even noticed.

How extraordinary! he thought, continuing on his way, a little more disheartened now, trying not to think about how hungry he still was. One bite of an apple, after all, is hardly a satisfying breakfast for an eight-year-old boy, especially one who's on his way to see the world and have a great adventure.

Chapter Two

The Second Village

It took much longer to reach the second village than it had to reach the first.

After what felt like a very long walk, in the distance Noah saw a large house with a bright orange roof, and it reminded him of a surprise day trip that his mother had taken him on a few weeks before, when they'd stopped for a cup of tea and a custard slice in a small café with roof tiles of the same startling colour. To his great delight, there was a pinball machine in the corner of that café and he'd scored 4,500,000 points on his first attempt, topping the leader board and sending the machine into a delirium of whistles and bells.

That was another achievement, he thought, remembering how happy he had felt at his triumph and how impressed his mother had been with him, particularly when she had a go herself and couldn't get past 300,000 points.

'Have you seen this?' she had asked the man who was standing behind the counter, wiping his glasses with a dirty cloth. 'My son just scored four and a half million points at pinball.'

'So?' said the man, as if anyone could do that.

'What do you mean "so"?' she asked, laughing a little and looking around in astonishment. 'He might become the world champion one day and then you'll be boasting to people about how he got his start right here in your café.'

'I don't think there is a world championship for pinball,' said the man, who looked like he hadn't smiled, or had anything to smile about, in a very long time indeed. 'It's not a proper sport.'

'Neither is the twenty-kilometre walk,' said Noah's mother. 'But they give medals for that at the Olympic Games.'

Noah had giggled at the time because he liked seeing his mother get so excited about something that he'd done, but he was surprised that it seemed to matter so much to her. (In fact, everything that day seemed to be very important to her. 'We can't waste a minute,' she told him when they left the café, looking around for more excitement. 'What can we do next?')

The second village was a lot busier than the first, as the sun had come up by now and the grown-ups were all going off to work, with that expression on their faces that said they'd much rather stay in bed for another hour and not have to go out at all. Most of them rushed right past Noah, carrying their briefcases under their arms, umbrellas in their hands because they always feared the worst, but one or two of them looked at him suspiciously, knowing that he didn't belong there. Fortunately it was still early enough that nobody was sufficiently interested to challenge him.

He looked up and down the street, wondering whether there might be a café there too – then perhaps he could play another game of pinball, and if he could achieve a high score that topped the leader list, maybe the owner would offer him a cooked breakfast to congratulate him on his magnificent achievement. He couldn't afford to buy one himself, of course, having decided not to steal any money from his father's wallet or borrow any loose change from his mother's purse before leaving home. Noah knew that it might have made things easier for him on his adventures, but he didn't want his parents' final memory of him to be as a thief.

He looked around but couldn't see anywhere offering the possibility of a free breakfast, and he felt a sudden rush of exhaustion sweep through his body on account of how early he had woken up and how far he had walked already. Without even considering how rude it might appear to anyone watching him, he stretched his arms out wide and allowed himself the luxury of a tremendous yawn. His eyes closed, his hands clenched into fists, and without meaning to, he punched a very short gentleman who happened to be passing by in the eye.

'Ow!' cried the very short gentleman, stopping

in his tracks and rubbing his injured face with his hand as he glared furiously at his attacker.

'Goodness!' said Noah quickly. 'I'm very sorry, sir. I didn't see you there.'

'Not only do you assault me, but you insult me too?' asked the man, his face growing red with indignation. 'I may be short but I'm not invisible, you know!' He really was the most extraordinary-looking fellow and not even as tall as Noah, who everyone said was a little small for his age but not to worry because that would all change one day soon. He wore what appeared to be a black wig on his head, but this had fallen on the ground at his feet, and when he retrieved it, he put it on his head back to front, making him look like someone who was walking away rather than getting closer. Before him, he was pushing a wheelbarrow containing a large grey cat, who opened his eyes for a moment, stared at Noah with an expression suggesting that boys like him were two a penny and hardly worth the bother, before promptly falling back to sleep.

'I didn't mean it,' said Noah, taken aback by the man's anger. 'Either the punch or the insult.'

'And yet you achieved both and have now delayed me. What time is it anyway?' Noah looked at his watch, but before he could reply the man let out a tremendous wail. 'Oh, tell me it's not that time,' he cried, his voice filled with fury. 'Oh my stars, we had an appointment at the vet's and he never treats late-comers. He kicks them right out onto the street instead. And if that happens, my cat is sure to die. And it will be all your fault. You really are a monstrous little boy.' His voice grew deep and loud as he said these last three words and his face turned the colour of an overripe turnip.

'I said I was sorry,' said Noah, a little surprised, for if the man was going to be late for his appointment, then he could hardly be blamed for it. He'd only stopped him for a moment, after all. And if the cat was going to die . . . well, cats died, and that was the end of it. His own cat had died a few months before and they'd given her a funeral and felt very sad about it but got on with their lives afterwards. His mother had even written a song on her guitar about the cat and played it as they covered the grave back over. She was good at doing things like that, Noah thought, smiling to himself. Not allowing sad things to ruin a day.

'Who are you anyway?' asked the man, leaning forward and sniffing the boy carefully, as if he was a bowl of whipped cream that had been left on the sideboard for too long and might have gone off. 'I don't know you, do I? What business have you got here? We don't like strangers in our village, you know. Go back to where you came from, why don't you, and leave us all in peace!'

'I'm Noah Barleywater,' said Noah, 'and I was only passing through because—'

'Not interested!' snapped the man, taking a firm hold of his wheelbarrow again and hurrying on his way, complaining loudly as he went.

The people don't seem very friendly here, thought Noah as he watched the man scurry away. *And I really thought this might be the right place for me to start over.*

But the incident left a sour taste in his mouth and from then on, as he walked through the village, he became convinced that everyone was staring at him and preparing to lift him clean off the ground and throw him in jail. And just then he caught sight of another man, of regular height, sitting on a bench reading a newspaper and shaking his head sadly, as if the continuing business of the world was a source of great disappointment to him.

'Heavens above!' cried the man suddenly, crumpling the edges of the newspaper in his fist as he stared in disbelief at the article he was reading. 'Oh my giddy aunt!'

Noah stared at him, and hesitated for only a moment before walking over and sitting down beside him, wondering what the man found so astonishing.

'That's shocking,' said the man then, shaking his head. 'Absolutely shocking.'

'What's that?' asked Noah.

'It says here that a quantity of apples was stolen from a tree in —' Here he named the first village that Noah had passed through that morning. '*The tree,*' read the man, '*was taking up its regular morning position when a young ruffian appeared out of nowhere and threw himself upon it, stealing three apples and causing a fourth to fall off a branch and become bruised upon the ground. Both tree and apples are being taken into hospital while their injuries are assessed. Doctors say the next twenty-four hours will be crucial.'*

Noah frowned. Although this news report bore a curious resemblance to his own adventure earlier in the morning, that had taken place no more than a couple of hours before, so it could hardly be possible that it was already being reported in the papers. And was it even news? His father said they printed nothing in those rags anyway, just a lot of pointless gossip about a bunch of people nobody really cared about.

'Is that today's paper?' asked Noah suspiciously.

'Yes, of course,' said the man. 'Well, it's the evening edition but I got an early copy.'

'But it's only morning time,' said Noah.

'Which is what makes it an early copy,' said the man testily, turning his head to look at the boy, before putting his glasses on for a moment and then taking them off again. 'Good heavens!' he gasped, his voice catching in fright.

Noah stared at him, unsure what had made him appear so frightened, but as he did so he caught sight of a drawing that was placed beneath the story of the apple thief. An eight-year-old boy, short for his age but with a fine head of hair. Taking a great bite out of an apple. *But how?* he wondered. There hadn't been anyone around to see him. A large block of text was printed in a bold font under the picture:

FOR MORE ON THIS STORY, SEE PAGES 4, 5, 6, 7, 14, 23 AND 40. PLEASE NOTE: THIS BOY IS A MENACE TO SOCIETY AND SHOULD BE APPROACHED WITH GREAT CAUTION OR NOT AT ALL.

I've been called worse, thought Noah, but the man beside him was having none of it because he let out a great cry at the top of his voice.

'It's him!' he cried. 'Stop him, someone. He's a thief!'

Noah leaped off the bench at that and looked around, sure that he would be apprehended at any moment, but fortunately for him, no one seemed particularly bothered.

'Stop him, someone!' the man shouted again as he ran away. 'Stop him! He's getting away with it.'

And that was the end of the second village, as far as Noah was concerned. He ran and ran until it had turned into nothing more than a great clump of buildings fading away in the distance behind him, and then it disappeared altogether and he couldn't remember what all the fuss had been about in the first place.

Chapter Three

The Helpful Dachshund and the Hungry Donkey

Things became a little more muddled after the second village. The path seemed to grow uncertain and the trees merged in front of him, then parted. The light finally broke through to allow him to see his way, then grew dim again and forced him to narrow his eyes to make sure he was walking in the right direction.

He looked down at his feet and was surprised to see that the crooked path had now disappeared entirely and he seemed to have wandered away from his original trail into a part of the forest that felt very different from everything that had come before. The trees were greener here, the air smelled slightly sweeter, the grass was thicker and more springy beneath his shoes. He could hear the sound of a running stream nearby, but when he looked around in surprise – for he knew that there was no water source anywhere near the forest – it became immediately silent again, as if it didn't want to be found.

Noah stopped and stood very still for a moment, glancing back in the direction of the second village, but it was impossible to see anything that far away. In fact, it seemed to have disappeared altogether, leaving nothing in its place but rows and rows of trees, which appeared to crowd together and block his view of what stood behind them. Somewhere through there, he was sure, was the path that he had been following since leaving home that morning. He had only veered away from it once, and that was when he had to run behind one of the trees because he was bursting to go. He thought about it for a moment and remembered that when he was finished and had turned round again to resume his journey, he couldn't remember whether he had approached the tree from the left- or the right-hand side, and so had simply chosen the direction that felt correct and continued on his way.

He wondered whether that had been a mistake. But there was nothing he could do now except keep walking, and within a few minutes he was relieved to see the trees begin to separate again in the distance and a third village appear before him. It was much smaller than the previous two and held only a small collection of peculiarly shaped buildings situated at irregular intervals along a single street. It was not quite what Noah was expecting to find, but he hoped that the people would be friendly there and that he might find something to eat at last before he passed out in a dead faint from hunger.

However, before he could take another step, his attention was taken by one curiously constructed building at the very end of the street, on the opposite side.

Noah knew one thing about houses: they were supposed to be built with straight walls all put together at right angles to each other, and with a roof sitting comfortably on top to stop the rain from making all the carpets soggy or the birds from doing their business on your head.

This building, however, was nothing like that.

He stared at it, astonished to see that every wall and window was entirely misshapen, parts coming out here, sections peeping out there, none of it making any sense at all. And while there was certainly a roof on top in roughly the correct place, it wasn't made of slate or tiles – or even thatch like his friend Charlie Charlton's house. In fact, it was made of wood. Noah blinked and looked at it again, cocking his head to the side a little and wondering whether it would look more normal if he looked at it askew.

But as curious as the building appeared to be, it was as nothing compared to the enormous tree that stood outside it, blocking his view of the sign above. Through the branches he could make out a few letters – a pair of Ns and an I in the first word, an O and a Y close together in the second, a final P in the third. He stared at it, trying to use his X-ray vision to see through the branches until he remembered that he didn't have X-ray vision – that was a boy in one of his books. But still, he wanted to read the sign and couldn't take his eyes off the tree. Without being able to say why, he found that it had entirely captured his attention.

Yes, it was tall, but no taller than many of the other trees that he had seen over the course of his life. (He did live at the edge of a forest.) They'd all been around for hundreds of years, or so he'd been told; it was no wonder they grew to such sizes. Trees, after all, were the opposite of people; the older people became, the smaller they seemed to get. With trees, it worked the other way round.

And yes, the bark was a healthy shade of brown, more like a block of rich, delicious chocolate than regular bark, but still, it was nothing more than the bark of a good, healthy tree and hardly anything to get over-excited about.

And it was clear that the leaves that hung from the strong branches were a lustrous shade of green, but they were no greener than any of the other leaves that fluttered in the summer breeze on trees around the world; no different to the leaves he could see on the trees that stood outside his own bedroom window.

But there was something extraordinary about this tree that he just couldn't put his finger on. Something hypnotic. Something that made his eyes grow wide and his mouth drop open as he forgot, for a moment or two, that he was

Fig 2

A strange TREE

supposed to keep breathing.

'You've heard the stories, I suppose?' said a voice to his right, and he spun round quickly to see an elderly dachshund trotting towards him, a half-smile on his face, accompanied by a heavy-set donkey who was looking around the forest floor as if in search of something he had lost. 'I can always tell when someone's come to take a look at her. You're not the first, young man. Won't be the last either. WOOF!' The dachshund let out a tremendous bark at the end of his remarks and looked away, raising his eyebrows haughtily with the air of a man who has just made a rude noise in a lift.

'I don't know anything about it, sir,' said Noah, shaking his head. 'I haven't heard any stories. I'm not from here, you see. I was just passing through, that's all, and I noticed the tree standing in front of that funny-shaped building and it grabbed my attention.'

'You've been standing in the same place for almost an hour,' said the dachshund, laughing a little. 'Didn't you know?'

'You haven't seen a sandwich around here, have you?' asked the donkey, looking up and fixing him with a stare. 'I heard rumours that someone had lost a sandwich here. It contained meat of some description. And chutney,' he added.

'I haven't, I'm afraid,' said Noah, wishing he had.

'I have a hankering for a sandwich,' said the

donkey in an exhausted tone, shaking his head sadly. 'Perhaps if I keep looking . . .'

'Don't mind him,' said the dachshund. 'He's always hungry. It doesn't matter how much you feed him, he still wants more.'

'You'd be hungry too if you hadn't eaten in more than twenty minutes,' sniffed the donkey, sounding a little hurt.

'Anyway, it's true,' continued the dachshund. 'You were standing there when I went for my run earlier, and I'm just back – I go through the fields and out to the well every day; it keeps me supple, you see – and here you still are. Staring at it.'

'Really?' asked Noah, crinkling up his face in surprise. 'Are you sure? I thought I'd just arrived.'

'That doesn't surprise me,' said the dachshund. 'People lose track of time when they start staring at that tree. It's really the most interesting thing in our village. Apart from the statue, of course.'

'What statue?' asked Noah.

'You mean you didn't notice it? It's right behind you.'

Noah turned round and, sure enough, a tall granite statue of a furious-looking young man wearing a pair of running shorts and a singlet stood behind him. His arms were raised in the air in triumph, and beneath his feet, carved into the stone, were the words, DMITRI CAPALDI: QUICK. It took Noah quite by surprise as he was sure it hadn't been there a moment before.

24

'Something sugary perhaps?' asked the donkey, stepping forward now and poking his nose so suddenly into Noah's pockets that he jumped back in surprise.

'Leave the boy alone, Donkey,' said the dachshund. 'He doesn't have anything sugary on him. Do you?' he asked quickly, narrowing his eyes at Noah.

'Nothing at all, sir,' said Noah. 'I'm quite hungry myself, as it happens.'

'It's very disappointing,' remarked the donkey, shaking his head and looking as if he might cry. 'Very disappointing indeed.'

'You know, there are those,' continued the dachshund, leaning forward a little now and lowering his voice, 'and I would consider myself of their number, who think that the tree is far more interesting than the statue. Which is why people stare at it for so long. I tend not to look at it myself if I can possibly avoid it. I missed a friend's birthday party once on account of it. Two years running.'

'You missed an excellent cake,' said the donkey slowly, allowing himself to smile at the memory of it, his large brown eyes welling up with tears. 'On both occasions it had frosted icing around the top. In the shape of roses. One year the icing was green, the next year orange. I can barely sleep for wondering what it will be this year. Do you think it might be red? I think it might. Or possibly blue . . . There's yellow too, of course,' he added after a long pause.

'Yes, yes, Donkey,' said the dachshund. 'There

are many, many colours in the world. We get it. Let's not exhaust our new friend's patience.'

'You're not hiding any pastries, by any chance?' asked the donkey.

'What's so special about the tree anyway?' asked Noah, ignoring the hungry donkey's question and turning back to look at the tree. 'I mean, there must be millions upon millions of trees in the world.'

'Oh no,' said the dachshund, shaking his head. 'No, that's a common mistake. There is in fact only one. They share a universal root, you see, at the very centre of the world, and they all spring from there, so strictly speaking, there's just the one.'

Noah considered this for a moment before shaking his head. 'That's not true,' he said, laughing a little at the absurdity of this statement, which led to the dachshund emitting a series of loud and prolonged barks, drooling and teeth-baring, which took several minutes to come to an end. The donkey merely looked away and sighed, investigating the grass beneath his nose for anything that might serve as a delicious snack.

'I do apologize,' said the dachshund, looking a little embarrassed when he had gained control of himself once again. 'It's just my nature, that's all. I don't like to be contradicted.'

'That's all right,' said Noah. 'Anyway, it seems like a very special tree, wherever it comes from.'

'It is. And I don't mind admitting it's the only tree in the village that I've never . . .' The dachshund blushed a little and looked around, as if he was nervous of being overheard. 'I mean, there are certain things a dog is encouraged to do *outdoors* that a boy is encouraged to do *indoors*.'

'I quite understand,' said Noah, giggling, not letting on that he himself had done it outdoors that very morning. 'So you've never . . . ?'

'Not once. Not in fifty-six years.'

'You're fifty-six years old?' asked the boy, opening his mouth wide in delight. 'Why, then we're the same age.'

'Really? You don't look a day over eight.'

'Well, that's because I *am* eight,' he replied. 'But in dog years . . . I would be fifty-six.'

The dachshund snorted loudly and the smile left his face. 'I call that a very rude remark,' he said after a moment. 'Why do you want to say such a thing? I've been friendly, haven't I? I haven't made any offensive remarks about your height. *Or lack thereof*,' he added dramatically.

Noah stared at him, immediately regretting what he had said. 'I am sorry,' he said, surprised by how personally the dachshund had taken his words. 'I didn't mean to offend you.'

'WOOF!' barked the dachshund, and then offered him a wide smile. 'Well, it's all forgotten now,' he said. 'And we are great friends again. But we were talking about the tree . . . Well, the interesting thing, of course, isn't really the tree at all.'

'It's the shop that stands behind it,' said the donkey.

Noah glanced beyond the trunk and looked at the misshapen building once again, which was now mostly hidden by the branches, as if they'd spread out in the intervening minutes to protect it from his inquisitive eyes.

'What's so interesting about that?' asked Noah. 'It looks just like a little run-down shop to me. Although I have to say I don't think the builders did a very good job on it. It's thrown together at sixes and sevens. I'm surprised a strong wind doesn't blow it over.'

'But that's only because you're not looking at it correctly,' said the dachshund. 'Look again.'

Noah stared across the road and breathed heavily through his nose, hoping that whatever his companion could see, he would see too.

'That shop's been here longer than I've been alive,' said the dachshund, sounding deeply impressed by what he was looking at. 'The elderly gentleman who lived there – he's dead now, of course – but he planted the tree by the door many years ago, just to brighten the place up a bit, you know. But the shop itself is much older than that.'

'Was he a friend of yours? The man who owned it, I mean.'

'A great friend,' replied the dachshund. 'He always threw me a bone whenever I was passing and I never forget such kindnesses.'

'You don't still have it, by any chance, do you?' asked the donkey.

'Afraid not,' said the dachshund. 'It was decades ago.'

'There can be good eating on bones,' said the donkey with conviction, staring at Noah and sounding almost animated now. 'Yes, some very good eating indeed.'

'The old man's son is also a friend, of course,' continued the dachshund. 'An excellent fellow too. He lived here as a boy, then disappeared out of all our lives for a very long time. But he came back in the end and he lives there still. WOOF! But my own father told me how the old man planted a seed and it turned into a sapling, and the sapling soon developed into a trunk that sprouted branches, and the branches sprung leaves, and before anyone on the town council had a chance to vote on it, this tremendous tree stood in the centre of our village.'

'It looks like it's been there for centuries,' said Noah.

'It does, doesn't it?' said the dachshund. 'But it's not quite as old as that.'

'Still, that's not such an unusual story,' said Noah. 'That's just nature. I mean, I learned all about nature at school, and there's nothing very strange about how well it has grown. The soil might just be very rich. Or they might have been fast-growing seeds. Or someone might have been pouring Miracle-Gro on them once a week. My mum does that, and once she found me pouring it on my head so I could grow taller, and she made me take all my clothes off and hosed me down in the back garden where anyone could see me. Although I was much younger then,' he added, 'and I didn't have much sense.'

'What a charming story,' said the donkey with a sniff that suggested he had no interest in it at all.

'And who said there was anything unusual about my story anyway?' asked the dachshund, offended again.

'Well, you did,' said Noah. 'You said there was something special about it.'

'Ah, but you haven't heard the best of it,' he replied, trotting in a circle around Noah now in his excitement. 'It's the most curious thing. Every few days something very strange occurs around that tree. The entire village goes to sleep and it looks exactly as it does now. And the next morning when we wake up, some of the branches have been stripped from it in the night, but there's no sign of any fallen wood. And a day or two later, they've all grown back! It's astonishing. I mean, it's the type of thing that happens in —' Here he named the second village Noah had passed through earlier that morning, before shivering a little, as if even the name of that terrible place left a sour taste on his tongue. 'But it's not the sort of thing we go in for here at all.'

'How extraordinary!' said the boy.

'Isn't it? WOOF!'

'And the shop. It's very colourful.'

'Well, of course it is. WOOF! It's a toy shop.'

The boy's eyes opened wide. 'A toy shop!' he said, gasping. 'My three favourite words!'

'Not mine,' said the dachshund. 'I like "a" very much, but I've never been much of a one for "toy shop". I've always quite liked the word "resilient" myself. An ability to weather trouble without succumbing. I feel that's a word you might think about a little, young man.'

'I like "fresh fruit flan",' said the donkey. 'Three excellent words.'

'I don't have one,' said Noah immediately before the question could even be asked, and the donkey opened his eyes wide in surprise, and for a moment Noah wondered whether he might even be considering eating him.

'I can see that I've lost your attention,' said the dachshund after a minute, sounding offended again as he tightened the scarf around his neck with his teeth, for the wind had picked up very suddenly and it was starting to grow cold. 'And we won't detain you any longer if that's the case. We shall be on our way. Good day to you, sir.'

'Yes, good day,' said the donkey, turning away with a sigh.

Noah offered a goodbye in return but it was less than it might have been, considering all the help the dachshund (and, to a lesser extent, the hungry donkey) had offered him, and a few moments later he found himself walking across the street. He stopped at the tree and reached out to touch it, but before his fingers could make contact with the bark, he thought he heard it growling at him, so he pulled away in fright. This wasn't the gentle whisper of the apple tree from the first village; it was something far more aggressive, like the snarl of a tiger protecting her cubs.

For a moment – for a very brief moment – he thought of his parents at home and how worried they would be when they discovered he had run away, which they surely would have by now. They wouldn't understand, of course. They would think him selfish. But the idea of staying . . . and watching . . . He shivered, knowing that he shouldn't think about such things.

He turned away from the tree now, trying to push his father and mother out of his mind entirely, and focused all his attention on the toy shop instead.

And the front door.

And the handle.

And without really intending to, he found his hand stretching out, grasping it, turning it, opening it, and before he knew it he was inside the shop and the door had closed firmly behind him.

Chapter Four

Puppets

Stepping inside the toy shop had not been Noah's original intention. All he really wanted to do at first was take a look in the window and see what was on display. He didn't have any money to buy anything, of course, but it didn't do any harm to take a look at what he couldn't afford. He also wanted to make sure that there were not too many customers milling around in case they realized he didn't belong there and called the village police.

But somehow he felt as if he had been sucked inside the shop without his making any decision at all, as if the whole thing had all been entirely outside of his control. Of course, this was most unexpected, but he felt that now he was here, the best thing to do was simply take a look around and see what the shop was like.

The first thing he noticed was how quiet it was. This was nothing like the kind of quiet he heard when he woke up in the middle of the night after a bad dream. When that happened, there were always strange, unidentifiable sounds seeping into his room from the tiny gaps where the windowpanes weren't sealed together correctly. At those moments he could always tell there was life outside, even if all that life was fast asleep. It was a silence that wasn't silence at all.

But here, inside the shop, things were very different. Here the quiet wasn't just quiet; it was a total absence of sound.

Noah had been inside a lot of toy shops in his life. Whenever his family went shopping for the day he made a point of being on his best behaviour, because if he was good, then he knew that he would be taken to one before they went home again. And if he was *very* good, there was even a chance that his parents might buy him a special treat, even if he was eating them out of house and home and they had no money to spend on luxuries. So it didn't matter if his mother insisted on his trying on every pair of school trousers in the shop before choosing the first pair she'd taken off the rack seven hours earlier, he still kept a cheerful smile on his face, as if shopping for clothes was quite the most exciting thing that an eight-year-old boy could do, and not something that made him want to scream at the top of his voice, so loudly that the walls of the shopping centre would break apart and every shopper, salesperson, cash register, rack, shirt, tie, pants and pair of socks would disappear off into the furthest regions of the solar system and never be heard from again.

But this shop was very unlike all the others he had ever visited in his life. He looked around, trying to understand what made it so different, and at first he couldn't quite put his finger on it.

And then he did.

The difference between this toy shop and all the others was that in this one there was absolutely no plastic to be seen anywhere. In fact, every toy he saw was made of wood.

There were train sets laid out along shelves, long, rolling carriages and tracks that stretched from corner to corner – all made of wood.

There were marching armies making their way forward to new countries and fresh adventures, and these were spread across counter tops – all made of wood too.

There were houses and villages, boats and trucks, every conceivable toy that an interested mind like his could dream of – and every one of them was made of a solid, dark wood which seemed to give off a glow of richness and, yes, even a sort of distant hum.

In fact, they didn't seem like toys at all, but like something far more important than that. Everything he saw on display was very new and different, and Noah had a sense that this might be the only shop in the world where these particular toys were sold.

Almost everything was painted carefully – and not with just any old colours either, like the toys he had at home, which had surfaces that cracked and peeled if he so much as looked at them for too long. These were colours he'd never even seen before; ones he couldn't possibly begin to name. Here, to his left, was a wooden clock, and it was painted, well, not green exactly, but a colour that green might like to be if it had any imagination at all. And over there, beside the wooden pencil holder, was a wooden board game whose overriding colour was not red, but something that red might look at enviously, blushing with embarrassment at its own dull appearance. And the wooden letter sets, well, there were those who might have said that they were painted yellow and blue, but they would have said this knowing that such plain words were an outrageous insult to the colouring on the letters themselves.

But as curious as all this was, as surprising and unusual as all this felt to Noah's eyes, it was as nothing compared to those toys that dominated the walls of the shop in such numbers.

The puppets.

There were dozens of them. No, not dozens, scores. Not even scores, but hundreds, perhaps more than a person could count in one day, even with the help of one of the multi-coloured wooden abacuses that were placed on a nearby counter top. They were crafted in different shapes and sizes, varying heights and widths, dissimilar colours and shapes, but every single one was made of wood and painted with bright colours that filled them with life and energy and a sense that they were fully alive.

They don't look like puppets at all, thought Noah. *They look too real for that.*

They hung in rows along the walls of the shop, wires fastened to their backs to keep them all in their places. And they weren't just puppets of people either; there were animals and vehicles and all sorts of unexpected objects. But they all had strings attached to them to allow their different parts to move.

'How extraordinary!' muttered Noah under his breath, and as he looked around, he began to experience a curious sensation that the puppets' eyes were following him wherever he went, keeping a close watch on his every movement just in case he picked something up and broke it, or tried to run off with a toy that didn't belong to him in his back pocket.

An incident just like that had happened a few months earlier when his mother had taken him on another of her unexpected days out – something she had started doing with such a sense of urgency that they should spend time together that Noah had found it all a little confusing. On that occasion, a pack of magic playing cards had mysteriously found its way into his pocket while they were walking through a shop together, but how it had happened was anyone's guess because he certainly hadn't stolen them. In fact, he couldn't even remember having seen them on display in the first place. But just as they were leaving the shop, a rather large, rather heavy, rather sweaty man in a pale blue uniform approached them and asked in a very serious voice whether they could come with him please.

'Why?' Noah's mother had asked. 'What's the problem here?'

'Madam,' said the security guard, using a word that made Noah wonder whether they had suddenly upped sticks and moved to France, 'I have reason to believe that your little boy might be leaving the shop with an item that has not been paid for.'

Noah had looked up at the man with a mixture of indignation and contempt. Indignation because he was many things – many things, indeed – but he was not a thief. And contempt because there was nothing that annoyed him more than grown-ups referring to him as a little boy, particularly when he was standing right there in front of them.

'Why, that's ridiculous,' his mother said, shaking her head dismissively. 'My son would never do such a thing.'

'Madam, if you could just check his back pocket,' said the security guard, and sure enough, when Noah put his hand round to check, the pack of magic playing cards had somehow found its way in there.

'Well, *I* didn't steal them,' insisted Noah, staring at them in surprise, the picture on the front of the box – the Ace of Spades – winking back at him in delight.

'Then perhaps you can explain what you're doing with them,' said the security guard with a sigh.

'If you have questions, you can address them to me,' snapped Noah's mother, glaring at the security guard, her voice rising a little now in indignation. 'My son would never steal a pack of cards. We have dozens of the things at home. I'm teaching him to cheat at poker so he can make his fortune before he's eighteen.'

The guard opened his eyes wide and stared at her. He was accustomed to parents turning furiously on their children at moments like this and shaking them until their teeth fell out to get at the truth, but Noah's mother did not look like the type of woman who would do something like that. She looked like the type of mother who might actually believe her son when he answered her questions, and that was something you didn't see every day.

'You didn't steal these cards, did you,' she asked, turning to him a moment later and phrasing it more as a statement than a question.

'Of course not,' said Noah, which was the truth, because he hadn't.

'Well, then,' said his mother, turning back to the guard again and shrugging her shoulders, 'there's nothing more to be said on the subject. An apology will do for now, but I think you should make a donation to a charity of my choice as recompense for your wrongful accusations. Something to do with animals, I think. Small furry ones as they're my favourite kind.'

'I'm afraid it's not as simple as that, madam,' insisted the guard. 'The fact remains that the cards were in your son's pocket. And *someone* must have put them there.'

'Ah yes,' she replied, taking them out of Noah's hands and smiling as she passed them over. 'But they are *magic* playing cards, aren't they? They probably leaped in by themselves.'

This was another happy memory. The type Noah tried not to think about. But that had been a very different shop to the one he was in now. There were no security guards here, for one thing. No one to accuse him of doing anything he hadn't. He bit his lip and looked around nervously, wondering whether he should go back outside and continue on to the next village, but before he could do this he became distracted by the sounds that were coming his way.

Footsteps.

Heavy, slow footsteps.

He held his breath and listened carefully, narrowing his eyes as if it might allow him to hear a little better, and for a moment the footsteps seemed to stop. He breathed a sigh of relief, but before he could turn round, they started again and he froze where he was, trying to identify exactly where they were coming from.

Beneath me! he thought, looking down.

And sure enough, there was the sound of

footsteps ascending from below the shop, the pounding beat of heavy boots slowly climbing a staircase, each one getting a little closer to where he stood. He looked around to see whether anyone else could hear them, but realized that he was entirely alone; until now he hadn't even been aware that he was the only person in the shop.

Excluding the puppets, that is.

'Hello?' whispered Noah nervously, his voice echoing a little around him. 'Hello, is anyone there?'

The footsteps stopped, started, hesitated, stopped, continued, and then grew louder and louder.

'Hello?' he said again, raising his voice now as every nerve in his body grew more and more tense. He swallowed, and wondered why he felt this curious mixture of fear and safety at the same time. This wasn't like the time he got lost in the woods overnight and his parents had to come and find him before the wolves ate him – now *that* was scary. And it wasn't like the afternoon he got trapped in the basement where the light didn't work because the latch had fallen on the lock – now *that* was just annoying. This was something else entirely. He felt as if he was supposed to be there but had better be ready for what came next.

He turned round and glanced back towards the entrance of the shop but – and this was a great surprise – he couldn't see the door any more. He must have wandered so far in that it was no longer visible. Only he couldn't remember walking that far at all, and the shop hadn't even seemed particularly big at first, certainly not big enough to lose yourself in. In fact, when he looked back, he couldn't see any way in or out of the shop, and no sign pointing towards the exit. All that stood behind him was hundreds and hundreds of wooden puppets, each one staring defiantly at him, smiling, laughing, frowning, threatening. Every emotion he could think of, good and bad. Every sensation. Suddenly he felt as if these puppets were not his friends at all and were moving, one by one, in his direction, surrounding him, trapping him inside an ever-decreasing circle.

'Who is he anyway?' they were whispering.

'A stranger.'

'We don't like strangers.'

'Kind of funny-looking too, isn't he?'

'Short for his age.'

'Mightn't have had his growth spurt yet.'

'Nice hair though.'

The voices grew more and more numerous, although they never rose above a whisper, and soon he couldn't make out any of the words at all, as they were all speaking at the same time and jumbling them up together into a language he didn't understand. They were closing in on him now, and he held his hands up in fright, closed his eyes, spun round and counted to three, thinking that none of this could possibly be happening and that when he took his hands away and opened his eyes again, he better just scream as loudly as he could and then surely someone would come and rescue him.

One,

Two,

Three—

'Hello,' said a man's voice then, the only voice to be heard now, for the chorus of puppets had become immediately silent. 'And who might you be?'

Chapter Five

The Old Man

Noah opened his eyes. It no longer felt as if all the puppets were crowding in on him, preparing to bury him beneath the weight of their bodies. The muttering had gone. The whispers had vanished. Instead they all seemed to have returned to their rightful places on the shelves, and he realized how ridiculous it was even to have thought they were watching him or talking about him. They weren't real, after all; they were only puppets. But what *was* real was the elderly man who had spoken to him and who was now standing only a few feet away, smiling a little, as if he had been expecting this visit for a very long time and was pleased that it had finally come to pass. He was holding a small block of wood in his hands and was chipping away at it with a small chisel as he stood there. Noah swallowed quickly out of nervousness and, without meaning to, let out a sudden cry of surprise.

'Oh dear,' said the man, looking up from his work. 'There's no need for that, surely.'

'But there was no one here a moment ago,' said Noah, looking around in astonishment. The door through which he had entered the shop was still nowhere to be seen, so where this man had appeared from was a mystery to him. 'And I didn't hear you come in.'

'I didn't mean to startle you,' said the man, who was very old, even older than Noah's grandfather, with a mop of yellow hair that looked like porridge mixed with maize. He had very bright eyes that Noah found himself staring into, but the skin on his face was as wrinkled as any the boy had ever seen. 'I was downstairs, working, that's all. And then I heard footsteps. So I thought I'd better come up and see whether a customer needed my attention.'

'I heard footsteps too,' said Noah. 'But I'm sure they were your footsteps, climbing the stairs.'

'Oh dear me, no,' said the old man, shaking his head. 'I could hardly have heard my own footsteps, then come up to investigate, could I? They must have been *your* footsteps.'

'But you were downstairs. You said as much.'

'Did I?' asked the old man, frowning and stroking his chin as he thought about it. 'I don't remember. It's all so long ago now, isn't it? And I'm afraid my memory isn't what it once was. Perhaps I heard the bell over the door ring.'

'But there was no bell,' said Noah, and at that precise moment, as if it had just remembered its job, a cheerful *ping* sounded from above the door, which had now reappeared a few feet behind him.

'It's old too,' explained the old man with an apologetic shrug. 'You wouldn't mind if it wasn't the only thing it had to do all day, but it forgets sometimes. That might not even have been you it was ringing for. It could be for a customer from last year.'

Noah turned round, open-mouthed, and stared at the bell in surprise before turning back and swallowing loudly, unsure what he could possibly say to make sense of what had just taken place.

'Anyway, I'm sorry I kept you waiting for so long,' said the old man, 'but I'm afraid I move like a snail these days. It's not like it was when I was a young man. You wouldn't have seen me for dust back then. Dmitri Capaldi had nothing on me!'

'It's all right,' said Noah, shrugging his shoulders. 'I haven't been here for very long at all. It wasn't even eleven o'clock when I came inside and— Oh!' He glanced at his watch, which told him that it was almost noon. 'But it can't be!'

'I'm sure it can,' said the old man. 'You just lost track of time, that's all.'

'A whole hour?'

'It happens. I lost track of a year once, if you can believe that. I put it down here somewhere, and when I went looking for it later, it was nowhere to be found. I always feel it will show up one of these days though, just when I least expect it.'

Noah frowned, not sure he'd heard this

correctly. 'How does someone lose track of a year?' he asked.

'Oh, it's easier than you might think,' said the old man, putting down the block of wood he'd been holding in his left hand and the chisel he'd been holding in his right as he took his glasses off and wiped the lenses with a rainbow-coloured handkerchief. 'Although perhaps it wasn't a year at all; perhaps it was an ear.' He pressed both hands to the side of his head and tugged on his earlobes. 'No, all in place there,' he said, sounding satisfied. 'It was definitely a year. Not to worry.'

Noah stared at the old man and tried to understand what he was talking about. None of it made any sense to him and he suspected that asking questions would only make matters even more confusing.

'It must have been all the toys,' said Noah, pointing at the walls around him. 'I was looking at them for a long time, I suppose. And all the puppets. There are so many of them, they distracted me.'

'That's right,' said the old man with a sigh. 'Blame the puppets! People always do.'

'I'm not *blaming* them,' said Noah. 'I just mean that I got caught up looking at them, that's all. They're so lifelike. And time ran away with itself.'

'The important thing is that you're here now,' said the old man, a great smile spreading across his face. 'Do you know, it's been so long since I had a

47

customer, I'm not even sure I know what to do with one. I'm afraid we have no official greeter any more.'

'That's all right,' said Noah, who always felt sorry for people who had to stand outside shops saying, *Welcome to . . . Welcome to . . . Welcome to . . .* It seemed like such a miserable way to pass the time.

'Of course, if I'd made it upstairs quicker, then I could have invited you to lunch, but it's too late for that now.'

Noah's face fell. His stomach was rumbling audibly and he had to cough to cover the embarrassing sounds it was making. Then he changed his mind, thinking that if the old man heard it rumbling, he might change *his* mind and feed him after all.

'Anyway, now that you are here,' continued the old man, 'I'm sure there must be a reason for your visit. Did you want to buy something?'

'Probably not,' said Noah, looking down at the floor and feeling a little ashamed. 'I don't have any money, I'm afraid.' A wooden mouse was sitting at his feet, painted grey and pink, sniffing a little at the toes of his shoes, but the moment he caught its eye it jumped a little, squeaked in surprise, and ran away to hide beneath the legs of a wooden giraffe in the corner of the shop.

'Then might I ask what brought you in here? Shouldn't you be in school?'

'No, I don't go to school any more,' said Noah.

'But you're just a boy,' said the old man. 'And boys should be in school. Or have they changed the law since I was your age? Not that I'm one to talk, of course. I spent very little time there myself. I was always running off. I can't tell you the amount of trouble I got into because of it.'

'What kind of trouble?' asked Noah, intrigued now because he always liked to hear about the trouble other people got into.

'Oh, I never talk about the past on an empty stomach,' said the old man. 'I haven't even had my lunch yet.'

'But you said—'

'Anyway, I want to know what brought you in here.'

'Well, at first it was the tree,' replied the boy. 'The one outside your door. I was standing on the opposite side of the street, just looking across at it, and I thought it was quite the most impressive tree I had ever seen in my life. I don't know why exactly. I just had a feeling about it, that's all.'

'I'm glad you like it,' said the old man. 'My father planted it, you know. The day we moved here. He was very fond of trees. He planted several others in the village but I think this is the best of the bunch. People tell the most extraordinary stories about it.'

'Yes, I think I heard one,' said Noah enthusiastically.

'Really?' asked the old man, raising an eyebrow.

49

'Might I ask where from?'

'There was a very helpful dachshund across the street,' replied Noah. 'And a very hungry donkey. He said that the tree is stripped bare every few nights and somehow manages to sprout new branches within a day or two. He said that no one knows how or why it happens.'

'Oh, he's full of stories, that one,' said the old man, laughing. 'He's an old friend of mine. I wouldn't mind what he says though. Dachshunds make up the most extraordinary tales. And as for that donkey . . . well, don't get me started. Where most people settle for twelve to fifteen meals a day, he needs to have three or four times that number or he gets weepy.'

'Twelve to fifteen meals a day?' asked Noah in surprise. 'I can assure you that I never have—'

'Anyway, for all the people who tell some tale about this shop,' said the old man, interrupting him, 'I can promise you that not one has ever set foot inside it.'

'Really?' asked the boy.

'Well, until now, that is,' said the old man, smiling. 'You're the first one. Perhaps you were sent here for a reason. Of course, my father died many years ago so he never got to see how tall and strong the tree grew.' A shadow fell across his face as he said this, and he looked away, unsettled for a moment, as if an unhappy memory had come over him.

'My father is a lumberjack,' said Noah immediately. 'He cuts down trees for a living.'

'Oh dear,' said the old man. 'Doesn't he like them then?'

'I think he likes them very much,' replied Noah. 'But people need wood, don't they? Otherwise there'd be no houses to live in or chairs to sit on or . . . or . . .' He tried to think of something else that was made of wood and, looking around, broke into an immediate smile. 'Or puppets!' he said. 'There wouldn't be any puppets.'

'That's very true,' said the old man, nodding slowly.

'And for every tree that he cuts down, he plants ten more,' added Noah. 'So it's a good thing really.'

'Then maybe one day, when you're as old as I am, you'll be able to walk past them and remember your father in the same way that I remember mine.'

Noah nodded but frowned a little; he didn't like to think of things like that.

'But I haven't introduced myself,' said the old man a moment later, extending his hand and offering the boy his name.

'Noah Barleywater,' said Noah in reply.

'It's a pleasure to meet you, Noah Barleywater,' said the old man, smiling a little.

The boy was about to say the same thing and opened his mouth, but then closed it almost immediately, for a wooden fly had been buzzing around his head just waiting for an opportunity to

Fig ~~✗✗~~ 3

An AXE in a
TREE STUMP

swoop inside. He remained silent for a few moments, but finally, after staring at the old man for so long he thought he could hear his own hair starting to grow, Noah searched his brain and found his next question hiding away just over his left ear.

'What are you making?' he asked, looking at the piece of wood the old man had picked up again and was chiselling away at even as they spoke, small flakes of wood falling at his feet and being gathered up and carried away by a wooden brush and pan that moved across the floor with the grace of a pair of ballroom dancers.

'It looks like some sort of rabbit, doesn't it?' said the old man, holding it up, and sure enough, it did look like a rabbit. With very large ears and a fine set of wooden whiskers. 'It wasn't what I was intending to make, but there we are,' he added with a sigh. 'It happens every time. I start out with one idea in mind and it ends up as something else entirely.'

'Why, what were you intending to make?' asked Noah.

'Ah,' said the old man, smiling a little and then whistling a little tune to himself, 'I'm not sure you'd believe me if I said.'

'Oh, I probably would,' said Noah quickly. 'My mother says I believe everything I'm told and that's why I get into so much trouble.'

'Are you sure you want to know?' asked the old man.

'Please tell me,' said Noah, intrigued now.

'You're not a gossip, are you?' he asked. 'You won't go around telling people?'

'No, of course not,' said Noah. 'I won't tell a single person.'

The old man smiled and seemed to consider it. 'I wonder if I can trust you,' he said quietly. 'What do you think? Are you a trustworthy little boy, Noah Barleywater?'

Chapter Six

The Clock, the Door and the Box of Memories

Noah didn't have an opportunity to tell the old man just how trustworthy he was, for just at that moment a clock that was standing on the counter next to him began to make some very strange sounds indeed. At first it was just a sort of quiet moaning, as if the clock wasn't feeling very well and wanted to go straight to bed and hide under the blankets until the pain passed. Then silence. Then the moaning transformed itself into a sort of *chugga-chugga-chugga* sound before settling into a series of curious and rather embarrassing rumbles, as if all the internal sprockets and springs were having a tremendous argument with each other and it could end in violence at any moment.

'Oh dear me,' said the old man, turning round and glancing at it. 'How embarrassing! You'll have to forgive me.'

'Forgive *you?*' asked Noah, surprised. 'But it's the clock that's making the noises.'

At that, the clock issued an offended squeak

and Noah started to giggle, putting his hand over his mouth as he did so. The noises reminded him of Charlie Charlton, whose stomach always started to make the strangest sounds when it was coming up to lunch time, and that was the cue for Miss Bright to look at her watch and say, 'Oh, my! Is it that time already? Time for lunch!'

But just as Noah started to laugh, the part of him that had told him he should run away from home made him hesitate and he felt guilty for even smiling. He hadn't laughed in such a long time, he felt like a hedgehog must feel after he's emerged from months of hibernation and isn't entirely sure whether the things that came naturally to him were things that he was supposed to be doing at all. Noah shook his head quickly, throwing the laugh out of his mouth and over into the corner of the toy shop, where it landed on a pile of wooden bricks and wouldn't be discovered again until late the following winter.

'That's a very unusual clock,' he said, leaning down to inspect it closer. As he did so, the second hand immediately stopped turning, and only when he stepped back and looked away did it start to move again, going faster now so that it could catch up with where it was supposed to be.

'Best not to stare,' said the old man, nodding wisely. 'Alexander doesn't like it. It puts him off his stride.'

'Alexander?' asked Noah, looking around and

expecting to see someone else in the shop whom he hadn't noticed before. 'Who's Alexander?'

'Alexander is my clock,' said the old man. 'And he's quite self-conscious – which is a little surprising really, for I have found that clocks tend to be a bunch of show-offs for the most part, always on the move, always ticking away as if their lives depended on it. But not Alexander. He'd rather we didn't take any notice of him at all, to be honest. He has quite a temper. He's Russian, you see, and they're a funny lot. I picked him up in St Petersburg, at the Winter Palace of the Russian Tsar. Quite a few years ago now, of course, but he still works a treat, especially if you talk politics or religion with him, because that keeps him very tightly wound.'

'Well, I didn't mean to offend him,' said Noah, who didn't know what to think about this. 'But he was making some funny noises, that's all.'

'Ah, but that's because it's lunch time,' said the old man, clapping his hands together in delight. 'He reminds me by pretending that his stomach is rumbling. It's his little joke. The Russians are quite hilarious, don't you find?'

'But clocks don't have stomachs,' said Noah, sounding puzzled now.

'They don't?'

'No. They have pendulums or balance wheels. And something called an oscillator, which vibrates and keeps the whole thing running correctly. My Uncle Teddy gave me a present for my last birthday, a box set called "Make Your Own Clock in Twenty-Four Hours". I spent two weeks trying to put it together.'

'Oh, really? And how did that turn out?'

'Not well. It's only right twice a day, and sometimes not even that often.'

'I see,' said the old man. 'But still, you seem to know a lot about them.'

'Yes, I like scientific things,' explained Noah. 'I might be an astronomer one day. It's one of the professions I'm considering.'

'Well, I'll have to take your word for it,' said the old man. 'I always assumed it was his stomach but perhaps I was wrong. Anyway, whatever the truth of the matter, it's time for lunch.'

'I thought you'd already had your lunch,' said Noah, whose heart was lifting a little at the idea of food. It had been so long since he had eaten, he was worried he might pass out altogether.

'I had a little snack, that was all,' said the old man. 'Some leftover chicken. And a garden salad. And a few sausages that might have gone off if I hadn't eaten them today. And a cheese sandwich. And a slice of cake afterwards for a sugar kick. But nothing that you could call a substantial meal. Anyway, I expect you're hungry, aren't you? You left home very early, after all.'

'How do you know that?' asked Noah in surprise.

'Why, by the condition of your shoes, of course,' he replied.

'My shoes?' said Noah, looking down at his feet and seeing nothing unusual there. 'How on earth can you tell what time I left home by my shoes?'

'Look at the soles,' said the old man. 'They're still a little wet and there are small blades of grass stuck to them, although they're beginning to dry now and are flaking off all over my floor. It means you must have been walking through grass not long after the dew had fallen.'

'Oh,' said Noah, considering this. 'Of course. I'd never have thought of that.'

'When you've gone through as many pairs of shoes as I have, you tend to take an interest in other people's footwear,' said the old man. 'It's a little quirk of mine, that's all. A harmless one, I hope. Anyway, that being the case, perhaps you'd like to eat something? I don't have much in but—'

'I'd love to,' said Noah quickly, his face lighting up. 'I haven't had anything to eat all day.'

'Really? Don't they feed you at your house then?'

'They do,' he replied after a slight hesitation. 'Only, the thing is, I left home before breakfast.'

'And why would you do that?'

'Well, there was nothing in the house,' said Noah, lying.

The old man stared at Noah as if he didn't believe a word of it, and the boy felt his face begin to grow red. He looked away and caught the eye of one of the puppets on the wall, who immediately turned his own head away, as if he couldn't stand the sight of a boy who told lies before lunch.

'Well, if you're starving,' said the old man finally, 'I suppose I'd better feed you. Why don't you follow me upstairs? I'm sure I can find something up there that you'll enjoy.'

He walked towards one of the corners of the shop, extending his right hand before him, and the moment he did so, a handle appeared in the wall and he twisted it, opening a door which led immediately to the foot of an ascending staircase. Noah's mouth fell open in surprise – he was sure that door hadn't been there a moment before – and he looked from it to the old man, and back to it, and back to the old man, and back to it again. In fact, this could have gone on for much longer if the old man hadn't put a stop to the madness.

'Well?' he asked, turning round. 'Aren't you coming?'

Noah hesitated for only a moment. From as far back as he could remember he had been told that it was a foolish boy who went into strange corridors with people he didn't know, especially when no one knew that he was there in the first place. His father had always told him that the world was a dangerous place, although his mother said he shouldn't frighten the boy and he just had to remember that not everyone who appeared to be nice really was.

'You seem hesitant,' said the old man quietly, as if he was reading the boy's mind. 'You're right to be. But I assure you, there's nothing to worry about here. Not even my cooking. I passed through Paris many times when I was a younger man and learned a few tips from one of the greatest chefs of his day, and if I say so myself, I can scramble an egg with the best of them.'

Noah wasn't entirely sure whether he was doing the right thing or not, but the rumblings of his own stomach echoed those of the clock, which was now staring at him with murderous intent, tapping a foot impatiently on the counter. Overwhelmed by hunger, he nodded quickly and ran forward, following the old man through the open door.

Inside, he found himself standing at the foot of a very narrow staircase and, like the puppets in the shop, the steps and the walls were all made of wood. There was a series of intricate carvings along the handrail and he touched them with his fingers, enjoying the sensation of the grooves against his skin. They were very even, as if they had been cut carefully into the wood and then smoothed down with a plane to prevent any accidental splinters. To Noah's surprise, the staircase did not go directly up, as it did in his own house, but around in circles, so he could barely see the old man as he turned in front of him, for they were only within sight of each other for a couple of steps at a time.

They climbed and climbed, going round and round and round, until Noah began to wonder just how high they could possibly go. From the outside, it hadn't looked as if there was more than one storey on top of the shop itself, but it seemed to be going on and on interminably.

'There's an awful lot of stairs to climb,' said Noah, his voice wavering a little as he tried to catch his breath. 'Don't you get tired walking up and down them every day?'

'More tired than I used to, certainly,' admitted the old man. 'Of course, when I was younger I could run up and down these stairs a thousand times a day and never worry about it. But things are different now. It takes me a lot longer to do everything. There are two hundred and ninety-six steps, actually. Or two hundred and ninety-four. The exact same number as there are in the Leaning Tower of Pisa. I don't know if you've been counting.'

'I haven't,' said Noah. 'But which is it, two hundred and ninety-six or two hundred and ninety-four?'

'Well, both actually,' said the old man. 'There are two fewer steps on the north-facing staircase than there are on the south-facing, so it really depends on how you make your approach. You've been to Italy, I presume?'

'Oh no,' said Noah, shaking his head. 'No, I've never been anywhere. In fact, this is the furthest I've ever been away from home.'

'I spent some very happy times in Italy,' replied the old man wistfully. 'I actually lived quite near Pisa for a time, and every morning I would race to the tower and run up and down the steps to keep fit. Happy memories!'

'You seem to have been to a lot of places,' remarked Noah.

'Yes, well, I enjoyed travelling very much when I was young. I couldn't keep my legs still. It's all different now, of course.' He turned round and looked at the boy. 'But I think you're getting tired of climbing, aren't you?'

'A little,' admitted Noah.

'Well, then,' said the old man, 'maybe we should stop here.'

The moment he said this, Noah heard the sound of heavy footsteps running up the stairs behind him and he held his breath nervously, for he was sure that no one else had been downstairs. He turned round, half afraid of who or what might appear, and then gasped, pressing himself against the handrail as the door through which they had left the ground floor came running past him, puffing and panting, its cheeks red with embarrassment.

'Apologies, apologies all,' said the door, pressing itself firmly into the wall in front of him. 'I got talking to the clock and quite lost track of time. He never stops when he gets going, does he?'

'That's quite all right, Henry,' said the old man, reaching out and twisting his handle. 'I'm afraid I can't afford a second door at the moment,' he added, turning and looking back at Noah with an apologetic smile. 'So I have to make do with just the one. It's terribly embarrassing, but business has been rather slow these past few decades.'

Noah didn't know what to say to this, and stood on the staircase for rather a long time before shaking himself out of his surprise and staring through Henry into a small kitchen, which was both clean and messy at the same time, if such a thing is possible. Looking down at the floor, however, he was astonished to see that there were only about a third as many floorboards as were needed, great gaps appearing between each one, large enough to swallow an eight-year-old boy, and he peered through them but could see nothing below except a great darkness. This was quite unexpected as there had been nothing untoward about the ceiling on the ground floor.

'Well, shall we go in?' asked the old man, stepping back and allowing the boy to enter first, manners being crucial to him.

'But the floor,' gasped Noah. 'If I walk in there, I'll fall right through.'

'Ah, yes,' said the old man. 'I should have explained. I had to use some of the floorboards last year when I temporarily ran out of wood for the fire. They weren't happy about it, I don't mind admitting, and it wasn't my finest moment. But anyway, the rest of them make up for the deficiency. Watch this.'

Noah opened his eyes wide as the old man walked into the kitchen without a care in the world, and as he did so, the floorboards all jumped into action, popping up and bouncing forward with each step so the gaps kept changing but the old man never fell through, for each floorboard slotted into position beneath his feet just in time for him to tread upon it.

'How extraordinary,' said Noah, shaking his head in surprise and deciding to try it for himself. This time, the floorboards did the same thing – jumped out of every place and landed under his feet before he could fall through to the darkness below – but they seemed noisier now, and Noah was sure he could hear the sounds of gasping breath.

'They're not used to two people,' explained the old man. 'They'll probably tire more quickly. We should probably go easy on them. Now – food, I think!'

A range of different types of food was laid out on the counter and Noah walked carefully towards them, licking his lips and feeling his mouth begin to salivate already, thinking just how delighted the hungry donkey would have been if he had been invited in to share it with them.

'Please,' said the old man, indicating the spread. 'Help yourself. Just take a plate and fill it with whatever you want. If there's not enough here, I'm sure I can find some—'

'No, no,' said the boy quickly. 'There's more than enough. Thank you very much, sir.' He felt a sudden rush of affection for his host, and a feeling of gratitude for his kindness. He filled a plate with cold meat, coleslaw, a bread roll, a chunk of Old Amsterdam cheese, a couple of hard-boiled eggs, some sausages, a strip of bacon, a little horseradish, and decided that would probably do for starters. A bunch of very juicy-looking oranges were squeezing themselves into a pitcher at the end of the counter and he waited for them to finish before pouring himself a glass.

'Well, don't say thank you, whatever you do,' snapped one of the oranges, now pressed into an exhausted-looking, squashed rind and lying in a bundle on the counter as it glared at the boy.

'Thank you,' said Noah, stepping away nervously. A wooden teddy bear with white hair falling into his eyes was sitting on the window seat, wearing a bright red wooden bow tie, and Noah considered sitting next to him to eat his food, but the bear let loose a low growl as he walked towards him and Noah stopped in his tracks, unsure what he should do next.

'Take a seat over here, my boy,' said the old man, indicating one of the two chairs that stood on either side of the kitchen table. He hesitated for a moment before picking up a fresh piece of wood and a thicker chisel with a sharper edge to it than the one he had been using downstairs, and started to chip away, carefully at first and then with growing confidence. 'Might as well have another go at this,' he said with a smile.

'What are you carving now?' asked Noah. 'Another rabbit?'

'I hope not,' he replied. 'Although as it never turns out the way I planned, who knows what will appear out of the wood? But no harm in trying again.' He settled into the other chair and put his hand to the base of his spine as he did so. 'Bad back,' he muttered when he saw the boy watching him. 'One of the drawbacks of growing old. I've got no one to blame but myself though. Should have stayed as I was. I suppose you think everybody grows old and I have no right to complain.'

'No,' said Noah, without a moment's hesitation. 'No, I don't think that for a moment. Not everyone grows old at all.'

The old man stared at him, thinking about the boy's words, but didn't ask any further questions. 'Eat,' he said after a moment, pointing at the plate that sat fully loaded in front of the boy. 'Eat, before it gets hot.'

Noah didn't wolf down his lunch, despite his hunger, as his mother always said he should have consideration for the other diners and not eat like a pig who hadn't been fed in a month. Instead, he chewed his food quietly and slowly, enjoying every mouthful of the spread, which was as delicious as any food he had ever tasted.

'I used to have an appetite like yours once,' said the old man. 'Not any more though. If I have a dozen or so meals a day now, that's generally

67

enough for me.'

'A dozen or so?' asked the boy, astonished. 'At home we only ever have three. Breakfast, lunch and dinner.'

'Oh dear,' said the old man. 'That doesn't sound right at all. Doesn't your wife know how to cook then?'

'My wife?' asked Noah, bursting out laughing. 'But I don't have a wife.'

'Don't you? And why is that? You seem like a pleasant enough sort of chap. You're easy enough on the eye. You don't smell too bad. Well,' he added, sniffing the air and considering this, 'actually, now that I mention it—'

'But I'm only eight,' said Noah. 'You can't get married at eight! Not that I'd want to anyway.'

'Really?' asked the old man. 'And why ever not, might I ask?'

Noah thought about it. 'Well, maybe when I'm *very* old I'll get married,' he said finally. 'Like when I'm twenty-five. There's a girl in my class, Sarah Skinny, who's my fourth best friend, and I expect we'll get married one day, but not for a long time yet.' He looked around and considered how small this kitchen was and how it appeared to be designed for only one. 'And what about you?' he asked. 'Aren't you married?'

'Oh no,' said the old man, shaking his head. 'No, I never met the right girl.'

'You live here alone then?'

'Yes. Although I have plenty of company. Alexander and Henry, for example, whom you met.'

'The clock and the door?' asked Noah.

'Yes. And there are others. Many others. I've lost track really. And I have my puppets, of course.'

Noah nodded and continued to eat his lunch. 'This is very good,' he said, his mouth filled with food. 'Sorry,' he added, giggling a little.

'It's all right,' said the old man, holding the wood away from him now and blowing the dust off it. He examined it, appeared pleased by what he saw, and carried on, his chisel making careful and precise incisions in the wood. 'There's nothing quite as satisfying as watching a hungry boy eat,' he remarked. 'So if you have no wife, I expect you live alone too?'

Noah shook his head. 'No, I live with my family,' he said, his fork stopping in mid-air for a moment as he thought about them. 'Or rather, I *used* to live with them,' he said, correcting himself. 'Before I left, that is.'

'You don't live there any more?'

'No, I left this morning. I'm off to see the world and have adventures.'

'Ah, there is nothing quite like a good adventure,' said the old man, smiling. 'I once went to Holland for the weekend and stayed for a year after getting involved in a plot to overthrow the government.'

'I can't imagine I'd get involved with anything like that,' said Noah, who wasn't in the least bit political.

'And your parents were happy for you to leave home?'

Noah said nothing for a long time and then looked down at his plate, his face clouding over, the food before him suddenly seeming far less appetizing than it had a moment before.

'You don't have to tell me anything you don't want to,' said the old man. 'I do know a little of what it's like to be eight years old, you know. After all, I was eight myself once.'

Noah thought about it for a moment. The man was so old, he was surprised he could even remember what it was like to be his age.

'Did you ever run away from home when you were eight?' he asked, looking up and swallowing hard, for there was something he didn't want to think about because if he did, he would only become upset. He had been trying not to think about it ever since he woke up that morning, but it had a terrible habit of reappearing in his toes and running all the way along his ankles and up his legs and into his back and racing up into his brain and then sending pictures to his eyes that he didn't want to see.

'I did a lot of things when I was a boy,' said the old man. 'And not all of them were very sensible.'

Noah quite liked the idea of doing things that

weren't very sensible and was going to ask the old man about them, but before he could he noticed a large wooden box sitting on the floor next to his feet. He was a little surprised he hadn't seen it when he had first sat down, for it was very ornate and looked like the sort of antique his mother always picked up and examined in shops and wished she could buy for their house. It had a carving of a puppet on the top, one that was quite unlike the puppets on the walls downstairs, and Noah bent down to examine it closer.

'Did you make this?' he asked, looking up for a moment, and the old man shook his head.

'Oh no,' he replied. 'No, not me. I'm not quite as good a craftsman as that. The detailing, as you can see, is quite superb.'

'It's wonderful,' said the boy, reaching a hand down and tracing the lines of the carving with his fingers. The puppet on the top of the box seemed like a very cheerful fellow. He had a long, cylindrical body and a pointed cap on his head. His legs were remarkably skinny and he didn't look as if he could stand on them for very long without collapsing entirely.

'You'd be surprised,' said the old man, as if he could read the boy's mind. 'If you use a very old tree to carve the puppets, then the wood is so strong it can last for an eternity if it's treated right. That puppet could probably run to the ends of the earth and back and it would only need a fresh coat of varnish at the end of it.'

'If you didn't make the box,' asked Noah, 'then who did?'

'My father,' replied the old man. 'A long time ago now. I haven't looked inside it for many years. There are a lot of memories in there, and sometimes it can be quite difficult to face the mementoes of the past. Even to glance at them can make you very sad. Or regretful.'

All this only served to make Noah even more intrigued by the contents of the box and he looked down at it, biting his lip, then looked up again, desperate to know what was inside.

'Can I open it?' he asked after a moment, deciding that the simplest thing was to ask the question straight out. 'Can I see what's inside?'

The old man opened his mouth to reply but then looked away, his expression confused, as if he wasn't sure whether he wanted his box of memories to be released to the world. Not wanting to disturb his host while he was deciding, Noah didn't say a word until the old man looked back and smiled, nodding his head a little as he did so.

'If you like,' he said quietly. 'Only take a care with what you find in there. Those things are very precious to me.'

Noah nodded enthusiastically and reached down to lift the box onto the table before him. He noticed now that the sides displayed carvings of the same puppet that was depicted on the top, surrounded by foreign-looking buildings that he was sure he had seen in his geography books at school. One of them looked a bit like the Eiffel Tower in Paris, another like the Colosseum in Rome. He placed both hands at the sides of the lid and raised it carefully, holding his breath as he did so, convinced he was going to find something extraordinary inside.

But to his great disappointment, all it contained was more puppets.

'Oh,' he said.

'Oh?' asked the old man. 'Is there something wrong?'

'Well, I thought there might be photographs perhaps,' said Noah. 'I quite like photographs. Or old letters. But it's just more puppets. Like the ones downstairs. They're very nice, of course,' he added, not wanting to sound rude as he picked one out and examined it carefully. 'Only I thought there might be something different in here, that's all.'

'Ah, but these are very different,' replied the old man, smiling at him. 'The puppets downstairs, well, they were all carved by me. But these are the last remaining puppets that my father carved. They're very precious to me. Like the great tree outside, they put me in mind of him. They're all I have left of him.'

'Well, they *are* very interesting, I suppose,' said Noah, growing a little more intrigued now. 'But don't you want to put them downstairs with all the other ones?'

'No, I couldn't do that,' said the old man. 'My father wouldn't have wanted it. Each one tells a story, you see. A very particular story. So they have to be kept together.'

'Well, I like stories,' said Noah with a smile as he selected one at random, a rather portly puppet of a woman with a series of chins and a furious expression on her face. 'What does this one tell?'

'Ah, that's Mrs Shields,' said the old man with a laugh. 'My first teacher.'

'You keep a puppet of your teacher?' asked Noah, raising an eyebrow in surprise. 'You must have liked school very much then.'

'Some of it,' replied the old man. 'Although it wasn't my idea to go at all. It was Poppa's. My father, I should say. But that's another story. I'm sure you're not interested in how I got here.'

'Oh, but I am,' said Noah quickly.

'Really?' asked the old man, his face lighting up. 'Well, all right then. But I'll keep it brief. And where should I start? That's the question. Back in the forest, I suppose.' He thought about it for a moment and then nodded quickly, as if he was sure that this was a sensible idea. 'Yes,' he said. 'Back in the forest.'

Chapter Seven

Mrs Shields' Puppet

It was my father, Poppa (said the old man), who decided that we should leave our comfortable cottage at the edge of the forest and move deeper into the woodlands. The trees there were so old, they provided much better material for the toys and puppets he carved every day, and he liked the idea of a new beginning too. That year, life had changed so much for us that when we heard of the village – a little past the first, just further on from the second – we thought it sounded like a perfect place to begin our new life.

I was only eight years old at the time, but I hadn't lived a conventional life so far. I had a mischievous quality, you see, not unusual in boys my age, and a history of finding myself in the centre of terrible scrapes. I always seemed to end up meeting unusual people who wanted to lead me into harm's way. I was the type of boy who could be walking down the road to pick up a bottle of milk and find myself transported to a carnival by a cruel kidnapper, or working as a servant for a man who wished me nothing but ill. Every time I released myself from one of these exploits I would make a promise to Poppa that I would never allow myself to be sidetracked again, but every time I made this promise, sooner or later I would break it. It's not something I'm proud of, but it's who I was and I can't pretend otherwise.

But when I turned eight I decided that I was going to try to be a good boy, and to mark this change in my fortunes, Poppa thought it a good idea to begin our lives over in a place where no one knew either of us.

'After everything that's happened,' Poppa told me as he explained his plan, 'I think a change is exactly what we both need. We can start afresh.'

And so one morning, before the sun rose, before the dogs woke, before the dew stopped falling on the fields, we made the journey through the forest, not stopping to talk to anyone along the way, and only came to a halt when we reached this village.

Poppa asked me whether it felt like home, and I didn't have to think about it for long. 'Yes,' I said. 'Yes, I think it does.'

The first person we met was a young donkey who had been disturbed by our arrival while eating the grass that ran along the village street, and once he had swallowed a few last mouthfuls, he ambled over to say hello.

'Thinking of moving here, are you?' asked the donkey, who looked pleased to see that a boy of around his own age might be living nearby, someone who might take him for the occasional ride across the nearby fields. 'I can highly recommend it. Hee-haw! I've lived here with my herd since I was born. There's about a dozen of us but I'm the best one if you're ever looking for a little gallop. I run faster. I'd never let you fall off. And I'm a better conversationalist too. Hee-haw! I don't suppose you have any sausages on you at all, do you?'

'It's very kind of you to suggest it,' said Poppa before I could answer, pulling me further along the street before proceeding to tap the ground with his walking stick at brief intervals, breathing the air deeply into his lungs, getting down on his hands and knees to touch the grass and the hedges that lined the path, before having a series of brief but informative conversations with the various wildlife that made their way along there on a regular basis, much to the dismay of the donkey, who I could see was hoping that we wouldn't change our minds.

'Your father wants to be very sure before deciding, doesn't he?' he asked me, ambling over and sniffing my pockets in a curious way, as if he was looking for something.

'Oh yes,' I told him. 'He's hoping that we can live here for ever.'

'Well, I do hope he chooses this village,' said the donkey. 'You will come and see me often if he does,

77

won't you? I'm the best one – did I mention that? And if you come, bring something to eat. You should never start a gallop on an empty stomach.'

It seemed that the village was the right one for us, because when Poppa returned to the spot where the donkey and I were standing, he nodded his head happily and threw his arms around me.

'This is the spot, my boy,' he said. 'This is the place for us. I'm sure of it. We can be happy here.'

'Hee-haw!' cried the donkey, delighted by the news. 'Hee-haw! Hee-haw!'

And so, without wasting any more time, Poppa set about building our new home, putting it together brick by brick with his own two hands, which was not the smartest idea he'd ever had, for however good he was with wood and a chisel, he was not quite so skilled at construction, and as things turned out the house looked a little unusual, with the walls not quite standing at right angles to each other and the windows jutting out in all directions.

'Never mind,' I said, once we were settled in above the toy shop, for I didn't want him to feel disappointed. 'As long as it stands up, that's all that matters.'

'I suppose so,' he said. 'And now we have to start thinking about your schooling.'

'We don't really have to, do we?' I asked.

'Of course we do,' he replied. 'You've missed so much education already – you'll fall far behind all the other children and you wouldn't want that, would you?'

'Not bothered,' I said, shrugging my shoulders, and Poppa frowned at me and shook his head.

'I thought you were going to be a good boy from now on,' he said, a note of disappointment sounding in his voice.

'I am, Poppa,' I agreed, remembering all the promises I had made. 'I'm sorry. Of course I'll go to school if you want me to. For a bit anyway.'

And so, before I could change my mind, Poppa visited the local schoolmistress, Mrs Shields, and enquired about a place for me in her classroom.

'Of course we always welcome new additions to our class,' she said, beaming across at us and allowing her cheeks to grow a little rosy, for Poppa was a handsome man and Mr Shields had run away to join the circus the previous September. 'And we have a few spare seats. We'd be delighted if your son was to join us. But won't your wife be coming in to discuss his education too?' she asked, leaning forward and twirling her hair into curls around her fingers. 'I do so like to involve all members of the family in such important matters.'

'I have no wife,' said Poppa, hesitating before continuing; it was complicated, after all, and he didn't want to cause any more difficulties for me than were strictly necessary.

'Well, it doesn't matter,' replied Mrs Shields, delighted to discover that there was no rival for her affections. 'We cater for all sorts here. We have a girl who lived in a jungle for the first five years of her life and still only speaks in a curious hybrid of English and monkey. Her name is Daphne. I'm sure you'll get along with her famously.'

'We'll see about that,' I said, unconvinced.

'And then there's a boy who used to be an elephant but managed to escape that life just before Christmas,' continued Mrs Shields. 'Something to do with a series of wishes, I believe. But he's still settling in and seems a little troubled, if I'm honest. He keeps trying to eat his lunch through his nose, which is terribly messy.'

'That's disgusting,' I said, and Mrs Shields stared at me, her expression growing a little more chilly.

'What a spirited lad,' she remarked.

The next morning, when I entered the classroom for the first time, every student immediately turned round to look at me: every boy, every girl, every desk, every chair. Even the blackboard, which was short-sighted, leaped off its hooks and came over for a good sniff, before running back to the wall, shaking chalk dust off its front as it muttered, 'No, he'll never do. He'll never do at all.'

'This seat is taken,' said a rather obnoxious fellow called Toby Lovely, who thought he was better than everyone else in the class. He always sat next to the teacher in an attempt to ingratiate himself with her, and now moved his books over to the empty desk beside him as I walked on.

'Terribly sorry,' said a homely-looking girl called Marjorie Willingham, who had pigtails tied up in a pink ribbon, causing a flurry of giggles from the girls sitting around her, 'but I'm afraid this seat is taken too. And don't speak to me, if you please. I don't care for small talk with strangers.'

I continued along the aisle, growing more and more despondent as boy after girl after boy after girl rejected me, but finally I reached the last row and looked down hopefully at the one remaining seat.

'You can sit here if you want,' said the boy sitting next to it, whose name was Jasper Bennett and who had a series of bumps and bruises spreading angrily across his face. He cleared off the desk and pulled over a second seat, and I sat down gratefully, turning to my new desk-mate with an appreciative smile. Jasper looked at me for a moment, blinking, taking me in, with great tears forming in the pools of his eyes. 'Everyone hates me too,' he said after a long silence.

'Jasper!' screamed Mrs Shields, slamming her duster down on the desk and throwing a piece of chalk at him, which bounced off his ear and fell to the ground before picking itself up and making its way slowly back towards the front desk. 'I've spoken to you before about talking in class, haven't I? Well, haven't I?'

'Yes, miss—' began Jasper, before Mrs Shields cut him off.

'Jasper!' she roared. 'No talking!'

It took me a long time to form any kind of friendships with the other children in the class, and this was mostly on account of the fact that I had not known them as long as they had known each other.

'We don't care for new boys here,' said Toby Lovely one afternoon, walking towards me and sitting down on the corner of my desk before picking up a wooden pencil box that Poppa had designed for me. 'Can't you go to school somewhere else? The class is against you as a whole.'

'But there isn't anywhere else,' I told him, shrugging my shoulders. 'This is the only school in the village. Unless you want me to go to school with the donkeys.'

'Well, it's an option, surely,' said Toby Lovely.

'I've promised Poppa that I'll come here every day from now on,' I insisted.

'Answer me back, will you?' he snapped, turning to all his friends, who immediately agreed that this was a tremendous insult, and waited until the lunch break to jump on top of me and bend my arms back and pull my hair on account of it. When I emerged from the pile I was covered in bruises and scrapes, a pitiful sight to anyone who caught sight of me on the road home. Even Jasper Bennett, who was no longer being bullied since the other boys had found a new fellow to kick around, had jumped on me, which just went to prove that you could trust no one in this world, or that one.

'This would never have happened if you'd stayed as you were,' Poppa told me later that evening when he was putting plasters on my wounds and a dab of disinfectant on my scabs to keep the infection out. 'You have to take more care now. You have to try to make friends with the other boys, not get into fights with them.'

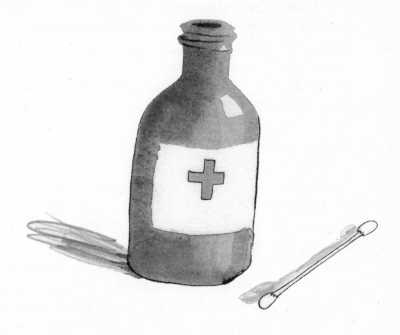

Fig 4.

A BOTTLe of DISINFECtant
and the MEANS of APPLICATION

The next day he went in to talk to Mrs Shields about the problem, and she told him that she would try to make sure that no one picked on me but that boys would be boys and there was really very little she could do about it. She said that if I wanted to have a happier time in school then I would have to stand up for myself, because in the end, nobody could help me but myself.

To be honest, Noah Barleywater (said the old man), it wasn't very helpful advice.

Chapter Eight

Noah and the Old Man

'So why did your father carve a puppet of Mrs Shields?' asked Noah, holding up the toy and pulling the string so a piece of chalk flew out from her hand a great distance before reeling itself back into the grip of her gnarly old claws.

'It was a gift, I think,' said the old man. 'He thought that if he was kind to her, then she might help me. But I think she thought it meant something more, which in turn led to a series of romantic misunderstandings – which are, I think, stories for another time. Anyway, she didn't help me much, that was the crux of it. But as it turned out, she was right. I did have to look out for myself. You probably have to do the same thing.'

'Me?' asked Noah, looking up in surprise. 'Why do you say that?'

'Well, aren't you running away from home because you're being bullied? It seemed like the most obvious explanation to me.'

'Oh no,' said Noah, shaking his head. 'No, I

have a lot of friends at school, although I'm sorry to hear that you didn't. There's a boy in our class called Gregory Fish, and he gets bullied all the time on account of the fact that he says all his Rs as if they were Ws.'

'Well, that's not very nice, is it?' asked the old man. 'You're not mean to him, I hope?'

Noah shrugged his shoulders and looked away. 'Sometimes,' he said, his face reddening a little. 'I don't mean to be.'

'Hmm,' said the old man, shaking his head as he chipped away at the piece of wood he held in his hands and then lifted it to the light to examine it carefully. 'And do you think you'll miss those friends of yours?' he asked.

'I don't miss them yet,' said Noah, thinking about the games they played together and the adventures they had. 'But I expect I will in time. They are very good friends, after all.'

'But still you ran away from them?'

'Who said I'm running away?' asked Noah.

'YOU DID!' roared the wooden bear in the red bow tie, who sat up for only a moment, pointed a finger at Noah and stabbed it dramatically in the air several times before collapsing down again into an inanimate state as if nothing untoward had happened. Noah stared at him, open-mouthed, before looking back at the old man in surprise.

'Something the matter?' asked the old man innocently.

'The bear,' said Noah. 'He shouted at me.'

'Yes, he can be terribly rude sometimes,' said the old man, shaking his head. 'I've warned him about shouting at strangers but it's in his nature, I'm afraid. There's nothing I can do about it. You might as well ask a squirrel not to sing along to the dawn chorus. Anyway, the point is, you are running away from home, aren't you?'

'Yes,' admitted Noah.

'And do you want to tell me why?'

Noah shook his head and reached into the box again, this time extracting a puppet of a man wearing a tracksuit. He pulled the string, and the whistle the man was holding in his left hand lifted to his lips and gave a quick, sharp *peep-peep* sound, although where he found the air to blow into it was anyone's guess.

'How extraordinary!' said Noah Barleywater.

'Ah, that's Mr Wickle,' said the old man with a laugh. 'If it wasn't for him, the things that happened to me in my life afterwards might never have happened at all. He was the one who got me interested in it, you see.'

'Interested in what?' asked Noah.

'In running,' replied the old man. 'I was a great runner as a young man, you see. You wouldn't think it to look at me now, making my way slowly up and down these staircases, but I was famous all around the world. And it was Mr Wickle who first realized how fast I could go.'

Chapter Nine

The Race

After a few weeks (said the old man) I began to
think it might be a good idea to give up school as a
bad job. I had no friends to speak of, and every day
Toby Lovely made things harder and harder for me.
One day he sawed off the legs of my chair, so that
when I sat down I fell to the floor and hurt myself.
Another day he put a bucket of varnish over the
door, and when I walked in, it fell all over me and
I had to have two baths in one week. He stole my
homework and ate my apples, tied the laces of
my boots together and mispronounced my name.
He said I came from outer space and had jelly
where my brain should be. He put a frog down the
back of my trousers and a ferret down the front,
which was actually more fun than he had imagined
it would be. Oh, I could go on and on with the
terrible things he did to me. He walked beside me
for a whole afternoon wearing a pullover with an
arrow pointing in my direction and underneath it
the words: I'M WITH STUPID. He spent every

Wednesday morning speaking to me in Japanese, at which he was actually quite proficient, and I started to pick up a few words. He poured salt in my porridge and put sugar in my sandwiches. He persuaded everyone in the class to wear hats for a day so that I was the odd man out. He sent me flowers and signed them with big kisses from someone called Alice. It was terrible, terrible, terrible. I started to dread going to school and didn't think that things could get any worse.

Until they did.

It was a Tuesday morning and Mrs Shields was going around the room discussing what jobs we all might like to have in the future, which might have been a little premature as we were only eight years old at the time, but she said we should all plan for our future, even at this early stage. She wanted to know not only what we wanted to be when we grew up but what our parents were now.

'My father is an international film star,' said Marjorie Willingham, 'and my mother is an astronaut. I hope to be a helicopter pilot.'

'Very good, Marjorie,' said Mrs Shields, nodding appreciatively. 'And you, Jasper Bennett. What do your parents do?'

'My father is working on a cure for the runny nose. My mother is a horse whisperer. And I have ambitions towards the priesthood.'

'And if you set your mind to it, you will achieve all your goals,' she declared happily. 'Matthew

Byron, how about you?'

'My father is the head of the armed forces,' said Matthew, 'and my mother helps people avoid paying income tax. I plan on being a professional footballer until I am thirty-four and a half, at which point I will turn my attentions to becoming the Poet Laureate.'

'So ambitious!' Mrs Shields smiled. 'Toby Lovely – I'm sure your parents are wonderful role models.'

'They are,' admitted Toby Lovely. 'You know those slides that go round and round and round, and when you come out the other end of them you land in a swimming pool?'

'I do,' said Mrs Shields.

'Well, my father invented them.'

'Fascinating,' said Mrs Shields. 'And your mother?'

'She invented swimming pools. That was how they met.'

'Of course. And how about you? What would you like to be when you grow up?'

'An athlete,' said Toby Lovely. 'I *am* the fastest boy in school, after all.' He smiled rather smugly, and received warm applause from the rest of the class.

'You are indeed,' said Mrs Shields, looking around carefully. 'Now, is that everyone? No one was left out?'

Every boy and girl in the class nodded except me, which I immediately regretted, for Mrs Shields noticed this and pointed in my direction.

'I do apologize,' she said. 'And what do your parents do?'

I swallowed nervously as I stood up. 'My father is a toymaker,' I said. 'Mostly puppets, but a few other things as well. He's very good with his hands.'

'Charming,' said Mrs Shields. 'Everyone needs toys. Well, until their late twenties anyway. And your mother, what does she do?' I was a little surprised that she was asking me this and bowed my head for a moment. 'Oh, of course,' she said. 'I'm so sorry. I forgot. You don't have a mother, do you?'

'No, miss,' I said, shaking my head.

'Did she die?'

'No, miss,' I said.

'Did she run away?'

'No, miss,' I said.

She seemed surprised by this and frowned. 'Well, where is she then? She couldn't have just vanished into thin air, surely?'

'I never had a mother,' I said.

'Never had a mother?' cried Toby Lovely, turning round to stare at me in amazement. 'I've never heard anything so ridiculous in all my life.'

'Then you haven't heard yourself sing,' I replied, astonished by my own bravery in standing up to him but leaving him lost for words, for he simply stared at me and began to seethe quietly.

I knew I wouldn't have heard the end of this, and sure enough, a few hours later in the playground, he came up to me and gave me a slap across the back of the head as a reward for my cheek.

'How does someone never have a mother?' he asked. 'It's not as if you were carved out of wood or something.'

'It's just one of those things,' I said. 'I never had a mother. You never had a brain. We all have something that makes us stand out from the crowd.'

And there it was again! Maybe it was the months of bullying that had led me to the point where I just felt I couldn't take another moment of it. Toby Lovely stared at me and laughed for a moment in astonishment before pawing the ground with his foot like a bull preparing to charge, and then jumped on top of me, the two of us rolling around in a great bundle of raised fists and pulling hair, as everyone else crowded around and cheered us on, delighted to see the all too rare spectacle of a great fight.

I lashed out in all quarters, and when we were finally separated – by Mr Wickle, the games master – I was delighted to see that I had given Toby Lovely a bloody nose; although not so pleased to feel the bruises on my ears and the blackened eye that was starting to bulge on my face.

'What's all this about?' asked Mr Wickle. 'Boys fighting in my playground? I won't have it! What are you fighting about anyway?'

I couldn't take it any more and roared at the top

of my voice: 'HE THINKS HE'S BETTER THAN ME! AND HE'S NOT!'

'Am too,' said Toby Lovely.

'Are not,' I countered.

'Am too,' said Toby Lovely.

'Are not.'

'Am too.'

'Are not.'

'All right, all right,' said Mr Wickle, silencing us both. 'That's enough, the pair of you. Look,' he said, turning to me. 'Toby Lovely is one of the brightest stars the school has ever produced. He won four gold medals on our last sports day, after all. He runs faster than anyone I know. If he says he's better than you at that, surely you can let him get away with it? Though as for you,' he added, turning to Toby Lovely, 'you should have more humility.'

'You're right,' said Toby Lovely, reaching across to shake my hand. 'I should simply accept my superiority and not look down my nose at others.'

'I could beat you in a race,' I said, shrugging my shoulders, not even thinking about the words before I said them.

Every voice in the schoolyard went silent when I said this, and remained silent for the best part of an hour. Finally, Mr Wickle's stomach started to rumble and we all shook ourselves out of it.

'For shame,' he said, shaking his head and looking at me with great pity in his eyes. 'That's an outrageous thing to say.'

'But it's true,' I said.

'It's not,' said Toby Lovely.

'Is too,' I replied.

'Enough!' cried Mr Wickle. 'If you think you are a faster runner than the most brilliant athlete the school has produced since the great Dmitri Capaldi, then there's only one way to prove it. We shall have a race!'

The school sent up a great cheer and, with extraordinary speed, separated down the centre into two ranks. The boys all stood on one side, the girls on the other, and they stared across at each other with their usual mixed expressions of fear and interest. Between them both, at the top of the lines, stood Toby Lovely and I, with Mr Wickle in between us. From the school itself ran Mrs Shields, carrying a pair of trainers.

'Toby's trainers,' she said, gasping for breath. 'He can't run without his lucky trainers.'

'Do you have your trainers with you?' Mr Wickle asked me, looking down at my hobnailed boots.

'No, sir,' I said. 'But it doesn't matter. He can wear them if he likes. I'll still beat him.'

'Fine, I will then,' said Toby Lovely, slipping them on, and we knelt down in our starting positions.

'Look ahead, boys,' said Mr Wickle. 'You see that apple tree in the distance? It's half a mile away. The first boy to bring me back an apple will be declared the winner. Are you ready?'

Fig 5.

A pair of HOBNail BOOTS
and another APPLE
(Note: No bite)

'Ready, sir,' we cried, and I wondered what I had got myself into, for I had never run a race in my life, let alone against someone like Toby Lovely, who was indeed a very fast runner.

'Set?'

'Set, sir,' we said, and I swallowed nervously, peering ahead towards the tree, deciding that whatever happened, I would try to give a good account of myself and not fall too far behind.

'Go!'

I raced forward, looking neither left nor right, completely unaware of how far my opponent might have been ahead of me, and when I reached the tree I grabbed an apple, spun round and raced back, popping it into Mr Wickle's outstretched hand, suddenly aware of how quiet the two rows of spectators had become. Turning round, I saw Toby Lovely only a few metres away, stopping, looking back at me in astonishment. He'd hardly even left his starting position and I'd been there and was back already.

'Good Lord,' said Mr Wickle, shaking his head. 'Now there's a surprise.'

Chapter Ten

Noah and the Old Man

'You won then?' asked Noah. 'You beat him?'

'I did,' said the old man, smiling. 'And believe me, I was just as astonished as everyone else. I never imagined I would win, but it turned out that I was a natural athlete, the fastest runner the village had ever known. And to be fair to Toby Lovely, he recognized this and congratulated me afterwards.'

'I suppose you became great friends after that?' asked Noah.

'Oh no,' said the old man, shaking his head. 'No, we couldn't stand each other. The bullying stopped, it's true, but we never spoke again. His story ends there, I'm afraid. But mine was only just beginning. The world was about to become my oyster.'

'And that's why your father carved this?' asked Noah, holding up the puppet of Mr Wickle. 'Since he was the man who helped the bullying come to an end?'

'Sort of,' said the old man. 'But Poppa wasn't

entirely fond of him, for he always said that if it wasn't for Mr Wickle, then I would have stayed at home in the years that followed and not kept running off and leaving him on his own. He missed me greatly, you see, when I was gone. We had moved into the forest in order for me to stop getting into mischief, but it seemed that I just found other sorts. He made this puppet so that he could stare at it and shake it in the air whenever he got angry with me.'

'How extraordinary,' said Noah as he put the puppet down on the table before him.

'You see, Mr Wickle immediately realized that my legs were unusually strong and signed me up for football and rugby, tennis and lacrosse, badminton and hurling, diving and parachuting, rafting and cycling, auto-racing and synchronized swimming, basketball and running, rock-climbing and rowing, sailing and archery, baseball and boxing, and soon I became known as the greatest athlete the village had ever seen. The polo teacher even invited me to sign up for polo classes but I shook my head at that.

'"No, I don't care for polo," I told him.'

'I've never known anyone who played so many sports,' said Noah.

'Yes, but I liked running best,' said the old man. 'Every day Mr Wickle would time me as I ran out of the school gates, along the road, into the forest and out again, up the street, across the village, past my friend the donkey and back to the schoolyard again, and he said that I had the most potential of any boy he had ever seen and he'd seen them all.

'"Here's a tip though," he told me, leaning over and pressing a hand into my shoulder. "If you want to improve your time, run faster."'

'That seems like good advice,' said Noah, considering it.

'Oh, it was. And faster I ran. Come the school sports day, I won every race on the card, and by the end of the day the other boys gathered around and put me up on their shoulders to carry me in a victory march through the streets, but thinking that they were planning on beating me up again, I ran away as quickly as I could – which was very quick – and never received the triumph. A few months later, the village's annual long-distance race, known as "the Long One", was held, and I won in a time that was fifteen per cent quicker than anyone had ever run it before. I ran it even quicker than the great Dmitri Capaldi, the legendary runner whose statue stood in the centre of the village. And when news of my success started to spread, the county board came calling, and before the year was out I was crowned the fastest runner in a fifty-three-mile radius. Not long after that I was named the fastest runner in the country. And that was when all my resolutions to be a good boy and stay with Poppa started to crumble, just like I had promised they never would.'

'I wish I had a skill like that,' said Noah Barley-water. 'I'm not much of a runner really. Although

I'm not bad at chess.'

'Hmm,' said the old man, thinking about it. 'Not really a sport though, is it?'

'It's a sport of the mind,' said Noah, sitting up straight and smiling.

'It is,' agreed the old man. 'But there'll be no one to play chess with now, I imagine. Now that you've run away from home, I mean.'

'No,' said Noah, looking down at the table again, concentrating on a knot of wood in the centre, scratching away at it with the nail of his thumb.

'I suppose it was your family then,' said the old man, standing up and clearing the lunch things away. 'They're the only people left. You must be running away from them. Now, what do you think of this?' he asked, holding up a puppet of an orang-utan, the result of all the carving he had been doing over the last hour.

'It's very good,' said Noah, taking it off him and examining it carefully. 'It's so lifelike. The way you've chipped the wood to look like monkey hair.'

'Yes, I suppose so,' he replied, sounding a little disappointed as he looked at it. 'It wasn't actually an orang-utan that I was trying to carve, but never mind.'

'Really?' asked Noah. 'What were you trying to carve then?'

The old man shook his head and walked over to a basket that sat in the corner of the room, overflowing with blocks of wood, selected one, examined it carefully, before nodding and sitting down again. 'It doesn't matter,' he said quietly, ignoring the boy's question as he picked up the chisel. 'I'll just try again. I'll get it right one of these days. I think there's a little dessert going if you'd like some?'

'If it's not too much trouble,' said Noah, who was still hungry. 'And I'm not running away from my family, by the way. It's just that . . . well, they're there and I'm here, that's all.'

'But they must be very bad people if you don't want to be with them,' said the old man, snapping his fingers for the fridge, who appeared before them in a very sprightly manner considering he was so full of sugar. He opened the door and looked inside. 'I'm afraid I don't have much to offer you,' he said. 'Just a little trifle, some jelly and ice cream, a chocolate cake, a banana cream pie and some cherry cherry double cherry flan. Will that do?'

'That will do nicely,' said Noah, who didn't like to think that the old man imagined his family were bad people and this was why he had left them behind. After all, they weren't bad people at all. They were very nice people actually.

'But if they're so nice, then why have you run away from them?' asked the old man, surprising Noah, for he was sure he'd only thought that in his head, not spoken it aloud.

'It's just better this way, that's all,' he said.

'Does your father lock you in the coal-shed?'

'No,' said Noah, appalled.

'Does your mother make you eat in the kennel with the dog?'

'Of course not,' said Noah. 'She'd never do anything like that. Besides, we don't have a dog. If anything, we always have great days out together, the two of us. Or we have over the last few months, anyway.'

'Oh yes?' asked the old man. 'That sounds intriguing.'

'Yes, well, there was the pinball café, for one,' said Noah, telling him the story of how he had scored the 4,500,000 points and topped the leader board. 'And then there was the time she saved me from the security guard who accused me of stealing the magic cards. And only a few weeks ago she built our own private beach.'

The old man raised an eyebrow in surprise. 'A private beach?' he asked. 'At the edge of a forest? That sounds unlikely.'

'You'd be amazed what my mum can do when she sets her mind to it,' he said, smiling a little. 'She's full of surprises.'

Chapter Eleven

An Unexpected Day Out

Noah's mother had never been the type of woman to do unexpected things, but this had all changed a few months earlier after their springtime holiday to Auntie Joan's was cancelled. They had gone there every Easter for as long as Noah could remember and he always looked forward to the trip, not just because they lived by the sea and Noah could spend hours splashing about in the water and making castles on the beach, but because his cousin Mark was his best friend, even though they only saw each other a few times a year. (The coast, where Auntie Joan lived, was a long way from the forest, where the Barleywater family lived.)

Everyone said that Mark was the opposite of Noah. He was tall for his age, and his parents told him they were going to put a brick on his head to stop him growing because he wasn't able to keep any clothes for more than a few months before he grew out of them. And he had a mop of blond hair, where Noah's was black. And he had blue eyes to

Noah's green. And he was a bit of a star at football and rugby, two games that Noah liked to play but wasn't very good at. For some reason he always got confused whenever they played them at school – football on Mondays, Wednesdays and Fridays; rugby on Tuesdays and Thursdays – and picked up the football and threw it sideways to the other boys on his team, or took aim at the rugby ball and kicked it into the back of the net, shouting '*Goooooaaallll!*' in a loud voice before running around the pitch with his shirt pulled over his head until he fell over. If it wasn't for the fact that the other boys in his class generally *liked* Noah, then there was a good chance they would have kicked him in after it.

'A slight change of plan,' his mother said one evening when the family was sitting down to dinner. 'Regarding Auntie Joan's, I mean.'

'We're still going, aren't we?' asked Noah quickly, looking up from his plate of fish pie, which he'd been moving around with a fork in the hope of finding something edible in the squishy mess that sat before him. (His mother was many things, but a good cook was not one of them.)

'Yes, yes, we're still going,' said his mum, looking around the table for salt and pepper to mask the taste rather than meeting his eye. 'Well, when I say we're still going, I mean we *will* be going. At some point in the future, that is. Just not next week like we planned.'

'Why not?' he asked, his eyes opening wide in surprise.

'A different week,' said his father quickly. 'We can go in the summer, all being well.'

'But it's all arranged,' said Noah, looking from one to the other in dismay. 'I wrote to Mark last week and we decided that on the first afternoon we'd go in search of crabs and—'

'The last time you went looking for crabs with Mark, you filled a bucket with them, and when one of them jumped out onto your arm, you dropped the lot on the stone floor of Auntie Joan's kitchen and they all ran away.' said his mother. 'Except for one unfortunate crab whose shell broke as it hit the floor. If anything, I imagine the crab population will be pleased to hear that you won't be visiting this Easter.'

'Yes, but I was only *seven* then,' explained Noah. 'Nobody knows how to behave when they're seven. But I'm eight now. I would treat the crabs with a lot more respect.'

'You mean you'd keep their shells intact before you dropped them, still breathing, in a pot of boiling water?' asked his father, who described himself as a bleeding-heart liberal and proud of it.

'I *would*,' agreed Noah. 'So can we go?'

'No,' said his mother.

'But why not?'

'Because we can't.'

'Why can't we?'

'Because I said so.'

'But why are you saying so?'

'Because it's not possible right now.'

'But why isn't it possible right now?'

'Because it isn't!'

'That's not an answer!'

'Well, it's the only answer you're getting, Noah Barleywater,' she snapped, and he knew that was the end of the matter, because his mother only used his full name when she had made up her mind on something and there was no turning back. 'Now eat your fish pie before it gets cold.'

'I hate fish pie,' grumbled Noah, who rather liked it actually when it was cooked right. (As in, by someone who knew how to cook.)

'No you don't,' said his mother. 'You always order fish pie when we go out for dinner.'

'I don't hate *real* fish pie,' agreed Noah, moving the pale pink and white slop around on his plate, some of the fish pieces looking so raw and inedible that a skilled veterinarian might have brought them back to life. 'But this, Mother . . . this – I mean, really.'

Noah's mum sighed. She knew that Noah only called her 'Mother' when he was absolutely certain of something and there was no convincing him otherwise. 'What's wrong with it?' she asked after a moment.

'It tastes like sick,' he said with a shrug.

'Noah!' snapped his father, stopping his own

fork from pushing the food around the plate for a moment to stare at his son. 'That's a terrible thing to say.'

'No, he's right,' said his mother with a sigh, pushing her plate away. 'I can't cook for toffee, can I?'

'You make quite good tomato soup,' said Noah, willing to give her that.

'That's true,' she said. 'I can open a can with the best of them. But my fish pie isn't up to scratch.'

'To be fair,' said Noah's father, 'it does look like something the dog would turn up his nose at. If we had a dog, that is.'

'Let's go out for dinner then,' said his mother, standing up and clearing the plates away. 'And you can order whatever you want.'

Noah smiled, the disappointment of the non-holiday forgotten for a moment, and jumped down from his seat, but just as he did so, his mother dropped the handful of plates she was holding, and all three fell to the ground, sending potatoes, prawns, cod, peas and all manner of squishy ingredients all over the floor. Noah jumped, expecting her to say that she was a terrible butterfingers, always dropping things, but instead she was leaning against the sideboard, one hand pressed to the small of her back, and was groaning quietly, a strange and disturbing sound, a heart-breaking cry that he had never heard her make before. Noah's father immediately jumped up and ran to her, and Noah stepped forward too, but there was no way over the fallen fish pie except to take a giant leap and he wasn't sure he could make it without taking a step back first.

'Go up to your room, Noah,' said his father before he could do this though.

'What's the matter with Mum?' he asked nervously.

'Go up to your room!' his father repeated, raising his voice now, and he sounded so serious that Noah immediately did as he was told, trying not to think about what was really going on downstairs.

And that, for the time being, was the end of that.

But then, two weeks later, on the day they should have been going to Auntie Joan's if the plan hadn't been changed, he was standing in front of his bedroom mirror measuring his muscles when his mother came marching in. She'd been sick in bed for a few days before that, but seemed to be better now and had been away all the previous day on what she described as a secret mission that he would learn about soon. 'There you are!' she said, smiling at him. 'How do you fancy a day out?'

'Love to!' replied Noah, putting down the measuring tape and making a note in his book of his current measurements. 'Where to this time? Back to the pinball café?'

'No, I have a much better plan that that,' she said. 'Since we can't go to the seaside, I thought we should bring the seaside to us. What do you think of that?'

Noah sighed and shook his head. 'We live on the edge of a forest, Mother,' he said. 'I don't think we'll find any beaches around here.'

'If you think I'd let a little thing like that stand in my way, then you don't know me at all,' she said, sticking out her tongue at him and making a face. 'You do realize that I'm the most amazing mother in the world, don't you?' Noah nodded but said nothing. 'All right then,' she said, clapping her hands together twice, and quickly, like someone in a television programme about to cast a spell. 'Grab your swimming trunks and a towel. I'll meet you downstairs in five minutes.'

Noah did as he was told, wondering what on earth could possibly have got into her. This was the second time she had taken him away for the day on an unexpected treat. The first time, the pinball time, had been the most terrific fun, and if that was anything to go by, then this would be even better. She never used to do things like this, but now, out of the blue, they were all the rage. Although he couldn't imagine how she could possibly bring the seaside to the forest. His mother was many things, but magic she was not.

'Where are we going?' he asked when they were sitting in the car, driving along with the top down for once. (In the past, Mrs Barleywater had said she didn't like to do that in case she got a cold, but she didn't seem to be worrying about that any more, and seemed happy to enjoy the fresh summer breeze. *You only live once,* she'd said as she pulled it down.)

'I told you,' she said. 'The seaside.'

'Yes, but in real life,' he asked.

'Noah Barleywater,' she replied, turning to look at him for a moment before turning back to watch the road, 'I hope you're not suggesting that I would let you down. You told me that you loved going to the beach.'

'Yes,' he said, 'but that's hundreds of miles away. We're not driving hundreds of miles, are we?'

'Oh no,' she said, shaking her head. 'No, I wouldn't have the energy for that. No, we should be there in about fifteen minutes.'

And sure enough, fifteen minutes later, having driven away from the forest and in the direction of the nearby city, they arrived at a hotel that Noah had never seen before and pulled into the car park. 'Don't say anything,' said Noah's mother, noticing the sceptical look on her son's face. 'Just trust me.'

They went inside, and Mrs Barleywater waved at one of the receptionists, who immediately came out from behind her desk wearing a broad smile on her face and handed her a key.

'Thanks, Julie,' said Noah's mum, winking at her, and Noah frowned in surprise, for he was sure he knew all his mother's friends and this Julie was a new one on him. He followed her as she walked on, however, only turning round for a moment to glance back at the receptionist, who was now standing with one of her friends, watching them walk away. She seemed to be shaking her head as if she was very sad about something, and she spoke to her friend, whose mouth fell open as if she'd just been told a terrible secret.

'Just down here,' said Noah's mother, holding his hand as they walked along the corridor. 'And through here. Do you want to press the button?'

Noah sighed and shook his head. 'You do remember I'm eight, don't you,' he asked, for when he was younger he always wanted to be the one to press buttons in lifts, 'not seven? Still, it needs to be pressed, I suppose.'

'B,' said his mother, and he pressed the button marked 'B', the doors closed and the lift slowly descended with a great many creaks and whistles.

'Where are we going?' he asked after a moment.

'Somewhere good,' she said.

When the doors opened again, they walked along another corridor, and Mrs Barleywater opened a door to an empty changing room. 'Run in there and put your trunks on,' she said. 'I'll change into mine next door. Quick sticks, now! Meet you out here in five minutes flat.'

Noah nodded, did as he was told, and five minutes later the pair of them were walking down another corridor until finally his mother stopped outside a door and turned round, smiling at him.

'I'm sorry we couldn't go to the beach this year,' she said. 'But I didn't want you to miss out just because of me.'

'What do you mean *just because of you?*' he asked, but instead of answering she simply unlocked the door with the key she had been given and they stepped through into the hotel's swimming pool area. Noah had been in pools before but never one like this. For one thing, there was no one else around, which was a big surprise in a hotel like this. Usually the pool was filled with middle-aged men splashing around in the water like whales as they powered their way through their lengths, or terrified-looking children bouncing nervously in the shallow end in case they lost their footing and the ground went from beneath them. But instead there was just the two of them, Noah and his mum.

But if he thought this was unusual, it was nothing compared to the way the swimming pool looked. Half a dozen small piles of sand had been brought in and built into dunes, and although it looked nothing like a real beach, it was probably the closest thing you could find at a swimming pool. Noah's mouth fell open in surprise and he looked up at his mother in wonder.

'All right, it's not *quite* the real thing,' she admitted. 'But we have the place to ourselves and we can pretend we're at the beach, can't we? One more beach holiday together. Let's make the best of it, shall we?'

DEEP END

Fig 6.

A SWIMMING POOL, WITH a
PILE OF SAND at one END

'Well, it's not just *one* more,' he replied. 'I mean, we can always go to Auntie Joan's next Easter, can't we? Or even later in the summer?'

Mrs Barleywater opened her mouth to reply but it seemed to take her an awful long time to find the words. She swallowed and looked away, and then leaned down and hugged Noah to her so tight that he thought she had gone mad.

'What's the matter?' he asked nervously, pulling away from her. 'Why are you acting so strange?'

'Me? Strange?' she said, clearing her throat and turning away from him. 'I don't know what you're talking about. Now, how about we take a swim?' she asked, walking over to the side of the pool. 'Race you to the other side.'

And with that, the two of them dived into the cold water and reached the other side almost neck and neck but it was finally agreed that Noah's mum had just edged it, although it was the only race she won for the rest of the afternoon, for Noah was a very strong swimmer and his mum seemed to get very tired quite quickly. Sandcastles were built, more swimming took place, and at just the right moment a picnic of sandwiches and fizzy drinks was served by a young man from the hotel staff, who seemed entirely unimpressed by what was taking place there.

'Well?' asked Noah's mother, throwing a few grains of the sand in his sandwich so it would taste even more like they were at the beach. 'Did you have a good time?'

Noah nodded quickly and looked at his mum, smiling widely. He wondered whether maybe she had some sort of allergic reaction to the chlorine in the water though, for her eyes seemed to be very red around the edges, as if she had been crying while she was in the pool. He was going to tell her that she should wear a pair of goggles in future, but his mouth was so full of egg sandwich at the time that he couldn't get the words out without spitting it all over her, and a moment later, when it wasn't, he'd already forgotten.

'We have to make the most of days like this, Noah,' she said quietly then, trying to pull him close to her again, but this time he pulled away because her swimsuit was too wet, and instead he jumped back into the water for another swim. He liked this new side of his mother, these unexpected days out. It was almost as if she was a different person.

Chapter Twelve

Noah and the Old Man

'Well, I've heard some things in my life,' said the old man, putting his chisel down for a moment. 'But I've never heard of a mother who made a beach out of a swimming pool before. What an extraordinary thing!'

'I told you she was full of surprises,' replied Noah.

'You did indeed. But I suppose it just makes me wonder why you're running away from her, that's all.'

Noah thought about this. 'Well, I'm going off to see the world and have a great adventure,' he explained. 'I don't think I need to go to school any more, do you? I'm very bright. In fact, I'm the seventh smartest in my class.'

'And how many are in your class?'

'Thirty,' said Noah, sounding quite pleased with himself.

'Well, that's something, I suppose,' said the old man quietly. 'But even adventurers need an education.

And even *great* adventurers like to go home once in a while.'

'Well, perhaps I'll go back one day,' said Noah, considering this. 'When I'm grown up, I mean. And when I've made my fortune.' He stood up and walked over to the mantelpiece, picked up a picture and stared at it. 'Is this your father?' he asked.

'It's a drawing I did of him when I was a boy,' said the old man. 'I keep it there so I won't forget what he looked like.'

'Does it look very much like him?'

'Not really, no,' admitted the old man. 'But I think I capture something of him around the eyes. Of course I don't really need it there. I feel he's here all the time.'

Noah frowned. 'Here?' he asked. 'In the toy shop?'

'Not physically, of course,' said the old man. 'But everything here reminds me of him in some way. He's a part of the place. It makes me happy to remember this.'

Noah put the picture back without a word, and when he looked up he found himself staring at his own reflection in a mirror. At least, he thought it was his own reflection, but after a few moments his face began to change. It grew a little longer, then wider, then better looking, then he had the beginnings of a beard, as if he hadn't shaved, then the beard was gone. A moment later he was wearing glasses and he looked quite handsome. Then he looked a little less handsome and there were wrinkles on his forehead. Then his eyes grew a little more damp and he had a moustache and his hair started to thin out and disappear. And finally, the face looking back at him in the mirror smiled for a moment before dissolving into nothingness and being replaced by his own eight-year-old face again, staring back in astonishment.

'How extraordinary,' said Noah Barleywater.

'What's that?' asked the old man, looking up from the table.

'The mirror,' said Noah. 'First it was me, then it was me looking a bit older, then it was a man, then it was an old man. Is it some sort of a game?'

'Not a game, no,' said the old man, walking over and looking at his own reflection, which didn't change at all; he remained an old man. 'Stop it, Charles,' he said, talking to the mirror. 'You'll frighten the boy.'

When he stepped away again Noah looked at his reflection once more, wondering what would happen next, but nothing did. It was just his own face, just plain old Noah Barleywater, nothing special, nothing dreadful, nothing to write home about.

'You still haven't told me why you're leaving though,' said the old man, sitting down again. 'Did your parents mistreat you?'

'No!' said Noah quickly, his face flushing red. 'No, it's got nothing to do with that.'

118

'Then I'm afraid I simply don't understand,' said the old man. 'After all, when I left my father, it was because I wanted to be a great runner and, well, time rather ran away with me. But you? You're not a runner, are you?'

'Well, I can run,' said Noah, mildly offended. 'I won the bronze medal in the five hundred metres at our school sports day last May.'

'The bronze, you say?' asked the old man. 'Third place, you say?'

'Third place is good!' snapped Noah. 'Out of thirty! There's no shame in third place.'

'Of course not,' said the old man. 'It's just not a position I'm accustomed to, that's all.'

'Well,' said Noah, looking away and feeling uncertain whether he wanted to tell the old man everything or just sit quietly in a corner and bury his face in his hands. 'My parents were never mean to me,' he said, trying to control the painful feeling that was spreading through his body and looking for a way out. 'I didn't like it when you said that.'

'Then I apologize for it,' said the old man, sitting down now on a three-legged stool that appeared behind him just in time to stop him from falling directly onto the floor. He picked up his chisel again to continue work on his latest puppet.

'It's all right,' said Noah, looking up and smiling a little before letting a great sigh escape. They stared at each other for a moment, their eyes locked together, before Noah looked away and pulled the craftsman's box over to him again. He reached inside and pulled out a puppet. It was of a handsome, slightly nervous-looking young man, wearing a golden crown on his head.

'Who's this?' asked Noah, looking up.

'A chap I once knew,' the old man said. 'A prince, if you can believe it. Of another country. A long time ago, of course. Back when I was a boy.'

'And your father made a puppet of him? Were they friends?'

'Oh no,' said the old man, shaking his head quickly. 'No, Poppa never mixed with people like that. In fact, he never left the village from the day he arrived here.'

'So why did he make a puppet of him?' asked Noah, pulling the Prince's string: the eyes rolled up in his head as if he was examining the sky.

'Because I met him,' explained the old man. 'He's an important part of my story. It was after the county board named me the fastest runner in a fifty-three-mile radius and I became very famous. I had an invitation to leave the village and demonstrate my skills elsewhere – my first – and I took it, promising I'd come straight back.'

'And did you?'

'Yes,' said the old man, nodding his head. 'Yes, on that occasion I kept my promise.'

Chapter Thirteen

The Prince's Puppet

News of my success as a runner (said the old man) began to spread to the villages that surrounded my own, and then to the towns that looked down their noses at the villages, and then to the cities that sneered contemptuously at the towns.

One afternoon, when I arrived back at the toy shop from school, I found my father sitting at the counter, painting the carriage windows of a locomotive he had been carving over the previous few days.

'Ah,' he said, looking up and breaking into a smile as he saw me running through the door. 'There you are at last. I was beginning to worry about you.'

'Sorry, Poppa,' I said, checking my watch. 'It took me longer than usual to run home today. Almost three minutes.'

'Well, the school is four miles away,' said Poppa. 'So really you shouldn't feel too bad about it.'

'But I usually do it in just over two,' I told him,

stretching my legs behind me and running on the spot so fast that the floor let out a great cry and begged me to stop. 'I'll have to train harder.'

'You train hard enough as it is,' said Poppa, reaching across the counter and picking up a large, cream-coloured envelope and handing it across to me. 'Now, here's a surprise,' he added. 'A letter came for you this morning.'

I stepped forward and took the envelope from him. I'd never received a piece of mail in my entire life so this was a terrific treat.

'Who would be writing to me?' I asked, looking up at my father in wonder.

'Open it and find out.'

I stared at the envelope for a moment, weighing it carefully in my hands, before running my finger carefully beneath the seal and taking out the single page that was contained within. I read it once to myself and then once aloud.

> *Dear Sir* (it said*),*
> *Their Most Gracious Majesties, the King and Queen, instruct you to attend upon Them on Sunday 13th October in order to display for Them the great gifts of running for which you have become famous throughout the land. Please arrive at the palace promptly at 10 a.m. on the morning of the 13th and ask for me at reception.*
> *Yours sincerely,*
> *Sir Carstairs Carstairs,*
> *Equerry to Their Majesties*

'The King and Queen writing to me!' I said, looking up at my father in astonishment. 'I can't believe they even know who I am. I'll have to accept their invitation, of course.'

'But you have school,' said Poppa. 'You can't miss out on your education just for a bit of running.'

'Oh, I could go just for a day or two,' I said. 'They wouldn't even know I was gone.'

'And what about me?' asked Poppa quietly, his voice filled with sadness. 'You will come back to me, won't you?'

'Why, of course I will,' I declared. 'I won't leave you all alone.'

'Do you promise?' asked Poppa.

'Yes, yes,' I said, smiling at him, scarcely even thinking about whether I meant it or not.

And so, on the evening of 12th October, I ran the hundred miles or so to the harbour and jumped aboard a boat that was headed in the general direction of the palace, and I was ready in the court-yard in my running clothes first thing the following morning when the King and Queen came out to take their daily constitutionals. Behind them loped a young man a few years older than me, with bright blond hair and a golden crown, his neck stretched right back as he stared up into the sky.

'Are you the boy they say is the tremendous runner?' the Queen asked me, holding to her eyes a pair of spectacles that she kept on a chain around her neck and looking me up and down as if she wasn't entirely sure she approved of me.

'Yes, ma'am,' I replied, nodding quickly. 'I can run faster than anyone else my age.'

'I'm the King,' announced the King. 'This is our son, the Prince. He will be King one day, of course, but not until I'm dead. He hopes that day will never come, don't you, my boy?'

'What's that, Father?' asked the Prince, taking his eyes off the sky for a moment and looking at the King.

'I said you hope that day will never come,' he repeated, raising his voice.

'What day, Father?' asked the Prince, entirely innocent of what was going on.

'Oh, for pity's—'

'Our son lacks concentration,' said the Queen then, interrupting her husband as she looked across at me. 'He is a great disappointment to us at present, which is why the King is being kept alive by extraordinary means. The Prince is simply not ready to be King.'

'It's true,' said the boy, shrugging his shoulders as he looked across at me. 'I'm not.'

'Well, I'm not sure what I can do about that,' I said, confused. 'I'm a runner. Perhaps you have me mixed up with someone else?'

'The Queen never makes a mistake,' snapped the King.

'I made one once,' she snapped right back,

staring across at him before returning her gaze to me. 'I know exactly who you are, boy,' she said, controlling her temper. 'You are the fastest runner in all the land. My question to you is this: are you strong?'

'Strong, ma'am?' I asked.

'That's right. Do you think you could run with the weight of . . . oh, I don't know . . . shall we say, a mouse on your back?'

I laughed, but stopped quickly as her expression turned to fury. 'Yes, ma'am,' I said. 'Yes, I could, most certainly.'

'What about a cat?'

'Without any difficulty.'

'A dog?'

'Cocker spaniels, no problem. Great Danes, not so sure. They might slow me down.'

The Queen seemed dissatisfied with my answer, breathing heavily through her nose in a manner that reminded me of a dragon. 'What if you had a boy on your back?' she asked after a moment.

'A boy, ma'am?'

'Must you repeat everything I say?' she asked, glaring at me. 'A boy. Yes, you heard me. Could you run with a boy on your back?'

I thought about it. 'I wouldn't be as quick as I usually am,' I told her. 'But I dare say I could do it.'

'Good,' she said. 'Well, quick sticks then. Put the Prince on your back and run him up to Balmoral. We've just invited one of the smartest men in Europe to set up house there and train our son in the art of kingship, and there isn't a moment to spare. The King is half dead as it is.'

'It's true,' said the King sadly. 'By rights, I shouldn't even be here.'

'And the boy has to be ready,' announced the Queen. 'Off you go now. No hanging around,' she said, waving her hand at me as the Prince jumped on my back and we prepared to start running. 'And bring me back my highland journal,' she added as we set off. 'I left it there on our last holiday and I wish to add a new entry.'

'And my rifle,' snarled the King, his eyebrows bouncing up and down furiously. 'There's a new stag in the park. Magnificent creature. Thing of extraordinary beauty. I want to shoot it.'

The Prince was lighter than I had imagined, and once I had grown accustomed to his weight I found that he didn't slow me down too much. I still managed to arrive in Scotland by late evening, and when we got there, to my surprise, the Prince didn't want to go inside at all but insisted on lying on the grass, staring up at the sky.

'Look up there,' he said. 'That's the Great Bear.'

'Where?' I asked, narrowing my eyes.

'There. The Big Dipper points north. Can you see it?'

'Ah yes,' I said, delighted, for I had never noticed it before. 'Of course.'

'And that's Perseus,' continued the Prince,

pointing out another set of stars. 'And over there is Cassiopeia, the Seated Queen.'

'You're interested in the stars then?' I asked.

'Very,' admitted the Prince. 'I'd like to be an astronomer, if I'm honest, but my parents won't let me. They say I have to be King.' He pulled a face, as if they had told him he had to go to bed early because they had a long journey ahead of them in the morning.

'Couldn't you just say no?' I asked.

'Impossible,' he sighed. 'If I don't become King, then the crown passes to my younger brother.'

'And what's wrong with that?' I asked.

'He's an idiot,' said the Prince. 'It would never work out. And after him it goes to another branch of the family, who we don't talk to. We'd be finished, the lot of us. My mother would never allow it.'

'So they've sent you here,' I said. 'To school, in a way.'

'In a way,' he said.

'I got sent to school too,' I told him. 'I didn't like it very much. But then it got better. When I realized I was good at something. Anyway, I'd better go inside,' I said, 'and fetch your mother's highland journal and your father's rifle.'

An elderly gentleman was waiting for me in the palace and looked at me with a mixture of irritation and fear, as if I had been sent to burgle the place. 'And who might you be?' he asked me, his voice echoing along the corridors.

127

I told him my name and what I was there for and he seemed to accept this as reasonable enough. 'I am Romanus Plectorum, late of Rotterdam,' he said. 'Is the Prince with you then?' he added, not sounding particularly enthusiastic.

'He's outside,' I told him. 'On the grass. You don't seem too happy to be here, if you don't mind me saying so.'

'I'm not,' he said. 'I've been summoned against my will to this awful place to tutor the boy. I'd just finished building a castle in Rotterdam with a glass roof so that I wouldn't have to spend any money on electricity. I would have saved a fortune. In my country I've become known as one of the foremost misers of our time. It's a great honour.'

'What about when it gets dark?' I asked. 'How would you be able to see anything then?'

'Candles, my boy, candles! It took me six years to finish the castle, and the day I moved in was the day I got the letter from the King and Queen. Now the castle with the glass roof is left empty, and who knows what will happen to it. And I'm stuck here. Here!' he roared, staring around in self-pity. 'Anyway, follow me. I'll show you where the Queen's study is.' He led me along a series of dark, wood-panelled corridors.

I stepped into an enormous office and took the book off the desk. Only when I looked up did I notice the number of stags' heads that lined the walls. Each one was more magnificent than the last, and

FIG 7

A STAG'S HEAD.
stuffed & mounted to a WALL.

they were nailed to wooden plaques with a date carved under each one – the date the King had shot them. I walked over and looked the animals in the eyes and was sure I could see the pain and suffering they had felt as they had collapsed, innocent, to the ground. I frowned and shook my head, noticing the enormous rifle that stood in the corner, the very thing that had caused so much unnecessary death.

'Here's your journal, ma'am,' I said to the Queen the following evening as I handed it across to her.

'They were right in what they said about you,' she replied. 'That was very quick indeed. And our son, the Prince – how is he? Was his tutor pleased to receive him?'

'Ah, that,' I said, wishing I'd had a little longer to prepare my story; one of the disadvantages of being a fast runner was that it didn't leave me a lot of time to think. 'Yes, they seemed to get along very well. Only they decided that Scotland wasn't the right place for him to be educated after all.'

'Not the right place?' roared the King. 'But the Scots are the second most intelligent people in the world, after the Irish.'

'Yes, well, that's as may be,' I said. 'But it's terribly cold and Mr Plectorum said he wouldn't last the winter, which would leave the Prince in an even worse position than he is now. They've gone back to Rotterdam to continue the Prince's education there. He said he'd write once they got there.'

The Queen grumbled a little at this news but said nothing.

'And my rifle?' snapped the King, dribbling a little into his beard as the taste of gunpowder and venison reached his lips. 'You didn't forget my rifle, did you?'

'Couldn't find it, sir,' I said with a shrug. 'Sorry!'

A low growl sounded from the King's throat and he looked as if he was about to attack me.

'I could go back if you really wanted me to,' I said nervously, knowing that even if I did, I still wouldn't bring the rifle back with me.

'Gracious no, boy,' said the Queen, shaking her head and loosening her wimple in the process. 'You've done enough. Anyway, we can't stand around here all day. The King has medication to take and the tourists will be at the gates soon. We have to start tearing up bits of bread to feed them with or they start to grow restless. How about you run around the palace once and I'll time you? Just for fun.' She removed a pocket watch from under her coat and held a finger above a large round button at the top. 'There's a rather lovely lavender bush at the back of the palace – you can't miss it. Bring me back a flower from it so I know you've gone all the way round.'

'One of these, ma'am?' I asked, holding out my hand and offering her a perfect purple sprig of lavender.

'Astonishing,' said the Queen, shaking her head.

'What can I tell you?' I said, smiling at her. 'I'm pretty quick.'

A couple of years later, I happened to be in Rotterdam for the Rotterdam Centennial Races and went to visit the Prince. It turned out to have been a very good set-up. He'd learned a lot at the hands of his tutor, but had done it on the glass roof of the castle, staring at the skies throughout. Really, everyone was happy. Even Poppa, when I arrived home.

'You're a day late,' he said, smiling at me but looking relieved nonetheless.

'But only a day,' I said.

'You came back,' he said, embracing me. 'That's all that matters. You kept your promise.'

Chapter Fourteen

Noah and the Old Man

'A boy in my class met the Queen,' said Noah, remembering the day Charlie Charlton had come into school wearing a suit and tie and with his hair combed straight for once in his life. 'He presented her with a bunch of flowers and said, "We're so delighted you could make the journey, ma'am." It was in the local newspaper.'

'Different queen,' said the old man, shaking his head. 'The king and queen I met are long gone now.'

He reached across, took the puppet from Noah's hands and looked at it fondly for a moment, running a finger along the carved design of the regal outfit before letting a great sigh escape his lips. He handed it back to the boy, who placed it flat on the table next to the puppets of Mrs Shields and Mr Wickle.

'It sounds like your father must have been very glad to have you back,' said Noah. 'Was he very lonely without you?'

'Well, of course,' said the old man. 'Parents

become very lonely when their children are away, don't you know that? And he didn't have many friends either. Of course, there was the donkey who had greeted us on our first day in the village. Although he was really more my friend than my father's as we were about the same age. And there was a dachshund too, who always stopped by for a chat. He and Poppa got along very well.'

'I met the dachshund this morning,' said Noah eagerly. 'He was the one who told me all about the tree outside your shop. He was very helpful. Although he seemed to take offence very easily.'

'Yes, he can be a little touchy, but he's a very decent dog, really. He's a particular friend of mine. In fact, the dachshund and the donkey are probably my closest friends these days.'

'My closest friend is Charlie Charlton,' said Noah. 'He can play the trombone and he started to teach me earlier this year, although he said I still have a long way to go if I'm to be even one tenth as good as him.'

'Well, that will never happen now, I don't suppose,' remarked the old man. 'Since you've run away, I mean. I can't imagine you'll meet too many strangers on the roads willing to give you trombone lessons.'

Noah nodded slowly and frowned. He hadn't thought of that.

'Anyway, the donkey and the dachshund were company of a sort for Poppa while I was away,' the old man continued. 'But I think I always knew that it wasn't the same as my being there to help out with the shop and play chess with him in the evenings. Parents can have all the friends they want, they can have every donkey and dachshund in the world come to visit them, but nothing makes up for not having their children near by. Why, I suppose your mother and father will be feeling that just now. They'll have noticed you've run away, I expect.'

'Yes,' said Noah, glancing at his watch. 'Yes, I expect they will.'

'And do they have many friends to keep them company?'

'A few,' admitted Noah. 'Although no animal friends. We don't go in for that type of thing at the edge of the forest. It's mostly humans who talk to each other back there.'

'Yes, I remember,' said the old man. 'That was one of the reasons I was so happy to move here when I was a boy. More variety. But still, if they have a few friends, like you say, then I imagine they'll forget all about you in time.'

Noah looked up in surprise, the words hitting him like a block of wood in the face. 'I don't think they'll forget me,' he said, feeling upset. 'I don't think they could ever forget me.'

'Not even if you never returned home?'

'I'd still be their son,' said Noah. 'Nothing can change that.'

'Perhaps they would have another son?' asked the old man.

'I don't think so,' said Noah, shaking his head. 'No, that's not going to happen.'

'Well, then,' said the old man. 'Of course I don't know them. I don't know anything about them other than what you've told me. But you're the one who's running away from home, not me, so I can only assume that you have a good reason for it.'

'When my mum cancelled the Easter holiday, I thought that was strange,' said the boy, looking down at the table. 'And when she turned the swimming pool into a beach, well, that was just downright odd,' he added. 'But I didn't think too much about it at the time. I thought she was just having fun. But after the fair—'

'Your mother took you to a fair?' asked the old man.

'Yes.'

'Well, that sounds like fun,' he said.

Noah nodded. 'It was,' he said, breathing heavily through his nose, for the memory of that afternoon still made him feel very upset. 'The day itself was very good. It was how it ended that ruined it.'

Chapter Fifteen

The Funny Turn

Mrs Barleywater showed up unexpectedly in Noah's schoolyard in the late morning, just after his class had been let out for lunch, and told him that he was to come with her because they were taking the afternoon off.

'We're doing what?' he asked in astonishment, for his mother had never allowed him to take time off school before, not even on the day when he didn't want to go in because he hadn't done his homework and had sat on a thermometer for five minutes to pretend that he had a temperature.

'A beautiful sunny day like this isn't made for school,' she said. 'We should make the most of the good weather, don't you think? I thought you and I could do something together.'

'But I have double maths in the afternoon,' said Noah.

'So? Do you like double maths?'

'No,' he admitted. 'Not even a little bit.'

'Well, then. Come on, let's go.'

'But my bag and my books,' he said, looking back towards the classroom and the headmaster, Mr Tushingham, who was marching their way with an outraged expression on his face.

'They'll all be there tomorrow,' she said. 'Quick now, before we're caught.'

They ran out of the school gates, hand in hand, as Mr Tushingham chased them to the car park, not liking what he was seeing one little bit, and he called out Noah's mother's name as loud as he could, sending the birds flying from the branches of the trees in fright, but she pretended not to hear him as she switched on the ignition and pulled out. And they would have made it too, only Mr Tushingham practically threw himself on the front windscreen so she had little choice but to stop and roll down the window with a sigh.

'Mrs Barleywater,' the headmaster said, panting and gasping for breath, for he looked like he hadn't taken any exercise since he was about Noah's age. 'What on earth do you think you're doing? It's the middle of the school day. You can't just drive off with the boy.'

'But the sun's out,' she said, looking up at the sky where the clouds had parted and a blanket of pale blue stretched into infinity above them. 'It's a sin to be stuck indoors on a day like this.'

'But it's against the rules,' protested Mr Tushingham.

'Whose rules?' asked Noah's mum.

'The school's rules,' he replied. 'My rules!'

'Oh, never mind about them,' she said, dismissing all this nonsense with a wave of her hand. 'Why don't you jump in the back seat too, Mr Tushingham? You can come with us if you like. No? Are you sure? All right, then. Goodbye!'

And with that she put the car into reverse and pulled out onto the road, driving down the street as Noah turned his head round from the back seat to see the headmaster standing with his hands on his hips, watching them disappear with a look of fury on his face.

'He doesn't look happy,' said Noah.

'Oh, I wouldn't worry about that,' said Mrs Barleywater. 'I'll write you a note for tomorrow. Besides, if I want to spend a day with my son, I will, and no school principal will tell me otherwise. We don't have a single minute to waste, you and I.'

Noah frowned. 'What do you mean by that?' he asked.

'By what?' she replied, looking up and catching his eye in the rear-view mirror.

'That we don't have a minute to waste.'

'Nothing in particular,' she said, shaking her head quickly. 'Only that life is short, Noah, and we should spend as much time as we can with the people we love, that's all. I think I've gone through my whole life without realizing that, but now . . . well, now it's suddenly become very clear to me. School will still be there tomorrow, there's no need

139

to worry about that. As will double maths. But today you and I are going to have a little fun.'

Noah decided not to argue with her because, after all, he was getting a day off and he hadn't even had to pretend to have a temperature for it, so he pulled his tie from around his neck, opened his collar and looked out of the window as they drove along. 'Where are we going anyway?' he asked when he realized they were driving along unfamiliar roads.

'There's a fair in the city today,' she said. 'I read about it in the morning paper and thought we ought to go and see it. It'll be quiet since everyone else is in school.'

'Brilliant!' said Noah.

They parked the car at the station and took a train into the city, and Noah's mum didn't even argue with the man sitting opposite them when he kept talking on his mobile phone, or with the woman on the other side of the carriage who kept making nasty sucking sounds with her chewing gum, because she said that sometimes it was easier just to live and let live. Instead she chatted away with Noah and they played train games together as if she was only eight years old herself.

When they got to the fair, though, she only went on one of the rides and left Noah to go on all the rest himself. 'But rollercoasters are no fun on your own,' he insisted. 'Please, Mum. We have to do it together.'

'I can't,' she said, not sounding quite as energetic as she had when they had driven away from the school that morning. Her voice sounded very tired and she looked like she had eaten something that didn't agree with her. 'I'm not feeling very well, Noah. But look, we're here to enjoy ourselves and I don't want to spoil it for you. Go ahead – you can have fun for both of us.'

'We could sit down for a few minutes if you want,' suggested Noah, pointing towards an empty bench behind them. 'Then go on something else together. You might feel better after a break.'

'It's probably best if you go on the rollercoaster alone,' she said. 'I'll watch you from down here, I promise. I'll wave up at you. Afterwards, I'll try one of the other rides with you if I'm feeling up to it.'

Noah wasn't very pleased with this but he didn't want to miss out on a journey on Space Mountain, so the next time it stopped to let passengers on he climbed into the front, hoping he wouldn't be left alone in it as he'd slide across the seat when the rollercoaster turned on its side, but then a little girl of his own age stepped in beside him, finishing some candyfloss as the attendant pulled the bar down in front of them.

'Hello,' said Noah, trying to be friendly. 'I'm Noah Barleywater.'

'I'm sorry,' said the little girl, giving him a sickly smile, 'only I'm not supposed to talk to strangers.'

And that was the end of that until the loop-the-loops began, at which point she grabbed his hand and screamed so loud in his ear, he thought she might shatter one of his eardrums.

The rollercoaster had been going much too fast for him to see whether his mum had been watching from the ground or not, and when he got off after three goes round, he was staggering a little from left to right, like his Uncle Teddy did every Christmas night when he left the house to make his way home. And when Noah finally got his balance back, she was nowhere to be found. He looked on either side, in front and behind, up and down the street, and frowned, biting his lip, wondering where she might have got to. It wasn't like his mum not to be where she had said she would be, and he didn't like the idea of going looking for her in case she came back in the meantime and was worried about what had happened to him. They might never track each other down again.

He sat down on the bench where he had left her, a forlorn expression on his face, and as he did so he saw a woman wearing a white uniform marching quickly towards him, her face all twisted up in concern. He didn't like the look of her at all and turned his head away, hoping she would pass him by quickly, but instead she stopped in front of him and bent down, just like he knew she would.

'Are you Noah Barleywater?' she asked.

'No,' he said.

'Are you sure?' she said, frowning. 'You look just

like the boy I've been sent to find. I was given a description.'

Noah said nothing, just looked at the ground, trying not to think about anything at all. Hoping the ground would swallow him up.

'Are you sure you're not Noah?' the lady asked a moment later in a more gentle voice.

'I am,' he admitted, nodding a little.

'Oh, good,' she said, her face breaking into a relieved smile. 'I thought you must be. Will you come with me?'

'I can't,' explained Noah. 'I'm waiting for my mum.'

'I know,' said the woman. 'She's had a funny turn, that's all. Nothing for you to worry about. She's waiting for you in the medical tent. She asked me to come and get you.'

Noah said nothing for a moment, sure that the whole world was conspiring in a secret he wasn't part of, but finally he agreed to go with her. The fairground woman tried to hold his hand as they walked along, but he made it very clear that he was having none of that sort of nonsense and put his hands in his pockets instead. Every so often he turned his head back to check the bench in case his mother had reappeared, but when he stepped inside the medical tent a minute later, there she was, lying on a bed with a doctor standing over her.

'Noah,' she said, sitting up immediately and trying to smile, but not making a very good job of

Fig 8.

An EMPTY BENCH.

either. Her face was very pale, almost grey, and there was a nasty smell inside the tent. It reminded him of how his own bedroom had smelled the night Charlie Charlton stayed over and ate too much chocolate and drank too many fizzy drinks and was sick all over the floor during the night. 'Sorry about this,' she said in a tired voice. 'But honestly, there's nothing to worry about. I just had a bit of a funny turn, that's all. It must have been all that candyfloss.'

'But you didn't have any candyfloss,' said Noah, staring at her, keeping a certain distance between them now.

They didn't take the train back home that evening, which was a shame as Noah quite liked trains. Instead they stayed in the tent for another three hours until Noah's dad arrived with the car and took them home again.

They were very quiet in the car during that journey, Noah most of all.

Chapter Sixteen

Noah and the Old Man

'So, if she hadn't eaten the candyfloss,' said the old man, setting the puppet he had been carving on the table half finished, then picking up the empty dessert plates and walking slowly across to the sink, where he turned the taps on, threw a couple of dishcloths in and let them get on with their work, 'why was she feeling ill?'

Noah looked down at the table and started running his finger across a dent in the wood that had been made, he assumed, by an out-of-control chisel. He didn't say anything, didn't look up, and hoped the old man wouldn't ask him any more questions of this sort.

'You don't want to answer me?' asked the old man eventually in a quiet voice, and Noah looked across at him and swallowed hard before shaking his head.

'I don't want to be rude,' he said, and as he spoke he found that his voice was coming out much more forcefully than he had intended, 'but now I've

146

run away from home, I think it's best if I don't think about my mum and dad at all. Or talk about them.'

'Well, now, that's a very strange thing to say,' said the old man, turning round and staring at him in surprise. 'First your mother stands up for you against a security guard who has wrongly accused you, then she makes a beach out of a swimming pool, and then she takes you out of school to go to a fair. And you don't want to talk about her? Why, if I'd had a mother like that . . . well, I never had a mother, of course, I only had Poppa,' he said sadly. 'But still, I don't understand why you don't want to be with her.'

Noah thought about this for a long time before answering. 'It's not that I don't want to be with her,' he said, growing more frustrated now. 'Oh, it's so difficult to explain! The thing is, she made me a promise, you see. And I think she's going to break it. And I don't want to be there when that happens.'

'You *think* she's going to break it?'

'Yes.'

'And what promise did she make?'

Noah shook his head, making it clear that he didn't want to say.

'Well, I'm very sorry to hear it,' said the old man with a sigh. 'Although I suppose we all make promises we can't keep from time to time.'

'I bet you've never done it,' said Noah.

'Oh, if you thought that, you'd be very wrong. You should have heard the promises I made when I was a boy. Do you know, everything my father ever did in his whole life was for my wellbeing, but time and again I let him down. Running off and having adventures, getting into all sorts of trouble. And if you want to talk about promises, well, I've had to live with a broken promise my entire life. Now, would you care for some tea? A cup of coffee perhaps?'

'I don't drink tea or coffee,' said Noah, making a face that suggested he'd just eaten a barrel of rotten apples. 'But I'll take a glass of milk if you have one.'

The old man opened the fridge and buried himself inside it for a moment, finally emerging with a frosted pitcher of cold milk, from which he poured a tall glass for Noah and set it on the table before him. He picked up his wood and chisel and started chipping away again.

Noah took a drink from the glass and then reached into the box again, selecting another puppet, and this one made him smile. He had a very thin body and a very square head; he looked like he had been based on a man who was composed of a set of geometric shapes rather than one with arms, legs and a torso.

'Ah, Mr Quaker,' said the old man when he saw it, laughing a little as he shook his head. 'I'm rather surprised that my father carved a puppet of him. Because if Mr Wickle was the man who got me interested in running, then it was Mr Quaker who

Fig 9.

A wooden CHEST,
open.

made me realize how many different ways I could use my gift. You talk about promises, Noah, but it was because of Mr Quaker that I broke one to my own father.'

Chapter Seventeen

Mr Quaker's Puppet

Soon after my visit to meet the King and Queen (said the old man), I returned home from school one day to be greeted by a most unusual sight: a customer standing in the toy shop talking to Poppa. I couldn't remember the last time this had happened – the donkey and the dachshund were generally the only visitors the shop ever received – and it was only when the bell over the door realized I was standing there and sounded a half-hearted ring that the man turned round and clapped his hands together in delight.

'And this must be your son,' he said in a loud and extravagant voice.

'This is him,' replied Poppa quietly.

'He's not as tall as I expected him to be.'

'Well, he is still quite young,' said Poppa. 'He hasn't finished growing yet. In fact, he's barely begun.'

'Hmm, I expect so,' said the man, marching forward and grabbing me by the hand before shaking it violently. 'Allow me to introduce myself. My name is Quaker. Bartholomew Quaker. Perhaps you've heard of me?'

'No, sir,' I admitted.

'Oh dear,' said Mr Quaker, his forehead disappearing into a series of frowns. 'That's a great disappointment. And a considerable blow to my pride. But never mind. I'm the official selector of the village team for this year's Olympic Games. You have heard of *them*, I imagine?' he added, turning round to Poppa and laughing heartily as if he had made a tremendous joke.

'No, sir,' I said again, shrugging my shoulders.

'You've never heard of the Olympic Games?' asked Mr Quaker in astonishment, leaning forward now and removing his spectacles in order to get a better look at me. 'You can't be serious!'

'We live a very quiet life here in the toy shop, Mr Quaker,' I told him. 'I'm afraid I don't get to see much of the outside world. Although recently I visited the King and Queen and—'

'But, my boy,' said Mr Quaker, interrupting me, 'the Olympics is the greatest sporting extravaganza the world has ever known. It exists to promote a sense of fellowship between nations and to celebrate extraordinary sporting achievement. Some athletes spend their whole lives training for the Games, and to win a medal is the pinnacle of their careers.'

'Well, it sounds like great fun,' I said, doing a

little running up and down on the spot to keep my blood circulating. 'I suppose you want me to take part in it, do you?'

'But of course!' said Mr Quaker, nodding his head. 'The news of your success as a runner has travelled far and wide. And it shames me to say that the village hasn't won a single medal since the days of the great Dmitri Capaldi. We're hoping that perhaps you'll be able to change all that for us. It's a great weight of expectation on the shoulders of one so young, but from what I hear, yours are quite strong enough to support it. What do you think? You won't disappoint us, will you?'

'If Poppa says I can go,' I replied, looking at my father for agreement, 'then I'd love to.'

'I'm not sure,' said Poppa quietly, the pain of impending loss already appearing on his face. 'They're held so very far away. And there's your schooling to think of. Wouldn't you rather stay here with me? I know it's not the most exciting life but—'

'We'll have him back before you even know he's gone,' said Mr Quaker, interrupting him, not wanting me to be discouraged. 'But tell me,' he added, turning back to me. 'You've only started running quite recently, I'm told.'

'That's right,' I said, nodding my head. 'Yes, I couldn't really run that fast before. My legs weren't up to it. But since I turned eight . . . well, things changed quite a bit for me.'

'Can I ask in what way?'

'My son doesn't like to talk about the past,' said Poppa, stepping out from behind the counter now and putting his arm around me protectively. 'Suffice it to say that before we moved to the village, my son was a very different fellow altogether. But when he decided to become a boy – a *good* boy, I mean; the boy he'd always wanted to be – well, since then he's realized that he has certain . . . gifts. The ability to run very fast being one of them.'

'Oh, you don't need to worry about that, sir.' Mr Quaker beamed. 'In my job, you meet all sorts and I never judge. I never make a judgement, sir,' he repeated as if he wanted to be very clear on this point. 'Do you know, I once worked with a boy who'd spent the first five years of his life trapped inside a pane of glass? He had extraordinary skills on the pommel horse and the parallel bars but sadly finished last in the qualifying heats, so that was a great disappointment. He was absolutely shattered afterwards. And in the last Olympics but one, another boy who had been expected to win gold in the chariot racing left his sense of humour behind on the train to the finals and was completely unable to concentrate during the event. He never came back, of course. He's still out there, trying to track it down, but he'll never find it. And I dare say you heard about Edward Bunson, from the next village along?'

'No, sir,' I said, my eyes opening wide.

'He was their great hope in the fencing competition,' recalled Mr Quaker with a sigh. 'But on the
day of the event he got a terrible case of the shakes
because he was so overwhelmed by the size of the
crowd who had come to see him, and he couldn't
go on. Those fields remained unfenced for years
afterwards. It was a tremendous shame.'

'There are worse things in life than failing to
win medals,' said Poppa. 'Youth is a prize in itself.
Why, I'm an old man now and my legs don't work as
they should. I have arthritis in my back. I'm blind in
one ear and deaf in one eye.'

'You have that the wrong way round, Poppa,'
I said, shaking my head.

'But I don't,' insisted Poppa. 'I don't, my boy!
And that's what makes it even worse.'

'This is all terribly interesting,' said Mr Quaker,
glancing at his watch, 'but I'm afraid I have a train
to catch and can't stand around all day making idle
chit-chat. I hope I can go back and tell my commit-
tee that you've agreed to take part? We'd consider
it a great honour.'

'I really would like to,' I told him, breaking into
a wide smile.

'But school,' cried Poppa in despair. 'Your
education!'

'Oh, you need have no worries on that score,
sir,' said Mr Quaker, tapping his stick on the ground
three times in rapid succession in such a way that
I stared at it, wondering whether he was about to

perform a magic trick. 'We make it a policy that for every one hundred minors on our team, we have a fully-qualified tutor on hand to give lessons. We take the education of our young athletes very seriously.'

'And how many boys will be travelling to these Games?' asked Poppa sceptically. 'Will there be others of his own age there?'

'Just your son,' said Mr Quaker proudly. 'Which means that we will have no need of a tutor and therefore save the expense, thus not wasting a penny of your hard-earned taxes, sir.' He leaned forward and banged a fist on the counter top. 'We are all winners in this scenario, sir, are we not?'

Poppa sighed and looked away, shaking his head in exhaustion. 'You really want to go?' he asked me a few moments later, staring at me as I performed a rousing set of calisthenics.

'Yes, of course!' I said.

'And you promise you'll come back?'

'I came back last time, didn't I?'

'You promise?' insisted Poppa.

'I promise.'

'Then, if it is your heart's deepest desire, I won't stand in your way. You must go.'

To everyone's astonishment I became the first person to take gold in the 100 metres, 200 metres, 400 metres, 800 metres, 1,500 metres, 5,000 metres and 10,000 metres in the same Olympic Games. I even took a silver in the 400-metre hurdles, but was so disappointed by that relative failure that I chose never to refer to it again, until now, and it was quickly removed from my official biography. And I became the only Olympian ever to win the 4 x 400-metre relay solo, by passing myself the baton in a complicated manoeuvre that quickly passed into legend.

No one could run faster than me; that was the simple fact of it.

As soon as the Games were over I remembered my promise to Poppa and thought it was probably high time I returned home, but that was when the exciting offers started to come in.

In Japan, the Emperor requested to see the boy who had deprived Japan's star athlete, Hachiro Tottori-Gifu, of so many medals at the recent Games, and I ran all the way across Europe, into Russia, down through Kazakhstan, across China and over to Tokyo to do a few circuits of the Imperial City for the Heavenly Ruler Above the Clouds. His own son, the Crown Prince, challenged me to a race, and although he was soundly beaten I was generous enough not to win by too large a margin. The Japanese, after all, were covering both my accommodation and all my expenses.

'Thanks very much,' I said afterwards to the cheering crowds. 'Now I'd better go home because I made a promise.'

But instead, I went to South America, where a group of freedom fighters invited me to take part in their twice yearly Lay-Down-Your-Arms Day, a celebration where all those on opposing sides of a particular political dispute came together for twenty-four hours and put on a sort of talent show. They made a point of inviting an international guest every year, and that year it was my turn. 'You think you very fast, don't you?' asked a general, puffing on a cigar after he had seen me run through the forests in record time. 'You think you big clever fellow.' He seemed a little offended by me, even though he had been the one to invite me.

'I do, sir, yes,' I told him, trying one of the General's cigars and promptly throwing up on my boots. 'But now I'd really better go home because I made a promise.'

But on the way home I found myself in Italy, where the Pope challenged me to run around St Peter's Square a thousand times in one afternoon. As the crowds gathered to watch and cheer me on, I found that I rather enjoyed the attention and didn't want it to end.

'Come into my private quarters,' said the Pope afterwards, putting an arm around my shoulders. 'Have a little tiramisu with me.'

'No can do, Your Holiness,' I told him, shaking my head. 'I really have to get home. I made a promise.'

And on the way, I found myself in Spain, racing with the bulls in Pamplona, then running north to Barcelona for La Diada de Sant Jordi, where I manned every book- and flower-stall in the city by chasing between them every time a customer appeared, and the entire city came to a standstill as I sped through the streets.

Closer to home, I found myself a little tired for once and decided to rest for a few days in West Cork, stopping off to be one of the judges in the Skibbereen Maid of the Isles Competition, an annual festival where every Irish man, woman and child descended on the town for twenty-four hours to run races, sing rebel songs and talk about the recession. I was invited to address the people, but I said I'd much rather show them how fast I was, and at that point a young woman in the crowd threw a set of keys at the stage.

'I think I might have left a tap running,' she said, giving me an address in Donegal, some three hundred miles away. 'Would you ever go up there and check it out for me, lad?'

'You didn't,' I replied a few moments later, throwing the keys back at her, along with a heavy red woollen jacket, 'but I thought you might need this coat later. It looks like rain on the horizon.'

'You're a credit to your mother and father,' the woman shouted back, and the crowd cheered again.

'Thanks very much,' I said. 'But I've no mother. Only a father. And I'd better be getting back to him quick smart. I made a promise.'

From there, I took a boat across to London, stopping for a couple of days at a literary festival, where I ran in and out of the authors' readings at such a speed that the wind I generated turned the pages of their books for them, leaving both their hands free for drinking and finger-pointing. And try as I might, no matter how hard I tried to get back to the village, it seemed impossible. There was always another crowd that wanted to see me, always another invitation to accept. Another festival to attend. Another race to run. Thoughts of Poppa were never far from my mind, though, and I tried to forget my promise to go home, even as I knew that the years were passing, my schooldays were already far behind me, and my father could not be getting any younger.

It wasn't until I had been sidetracked to St Petersburg and was running like a hamster in a giant wheel for the entertainment of the Tsar and his wife, the Empress of Russia, without ever taking a break or growing tired, that matters came to a head. A letter arrived for me, and I stopped running and stepped out of the hamster wheel. I read the words over and over, and felt the tears begin to spring from behind my eyes. I asked a young imperial bodyguard about the times of the trains from St Petersburg and was told that they were terribly slow, terribly rare and terribly cold.

'But I have to get home,' I said. 'My father is dying.'

'I'm sorry,' said the young guard, shrugging his shoulders and looking genuinely regretful that he could not be more helpful. 'But there are no trains.'

Fig 10.

The OPENED LETTer

'Then I'd better run,' I told him. 'And I promise that this time no one will get in my way.'

And that, at least, was a promise I kept.

Chapter Eighteen

Noah and the Old Man

'You were lucky to have a father like Poppa,' said Noah. 'If I wanted to do something like that, I'm sure my parents would never allow it.'

'You don't know that,' said the old man. 'Have you ever asked them?'

'Well, no,' admitted Noah. 'But then no one's ever come knocking on our door asking me to join the Olympics team. I'm only eight, after all.'

'And you only won the bronze medal in the five hundred metres at school.'

'Third place is good!' insisted Noah. 'Why do you keep saying that?'

'Anyway, I wasn't much older than you are when Mr Quaker came calling,' said the old man with a shrug. 'Still, different times, I suppose.'

The boy sighed and placed the puppet of Mr Quaker on the table next to those of the Prince, Mr Wickle and Mrs Shields. They lay there, staring up at him, not looking at all comfortable in such close proximity to each other. Noah thought they had been sitting in that box together for so long that they might welcome a little freedom but they didn't look happy about it.'

Without warning, a cuckoo flew in the open window, stopped in mid-air between Noah and the old man, glanced at them both for a moment or two, sounded a quick *cheep-cheep*, then flew right back out again and disappeared into a cloud.

'Oh dear me,' said the old man, consulting his watch. 'It can't be that time already, surely?'

'The cuckoo,' said Noah, jumping up and poking his head out of the window to see where the bird had flown off to. 'Does he do that every hour? Announce the time, I mean.'

'Of course,' said the old man, staring at Noah as if it was the most natural thing in the world. 'He's a cuckoo clock. You have those where you come from, surely?'

'Well, yes,' said Noah. 'We have one on our living-room wall at home, right next to the picture of Auntie Joan, but it's nothing like that. I didn't know they did that in real life.'

'Oh yes, if they're trained correctly. He's actually the second cuckoo clock I've had,' said the old man, looking a little regretful. 'His father used to do the job for many years but he met with a rather unfortunate accident one day when I forgot to leave the window open.' He hesitated for a moment, then raised the palms of his hands wide. 'Splat!' he said, shaking his head in dismay. 'I was very sorry about it and thought it was the end of matters between me and that family, but fortunately his youngest son realized that it was an accident on my part and forgave me. He's been coming here ever since.'

'And does he wake you up in the mornings?'

'Well, he tries to,' said the old man. 'Although I'm usually awake before he gets here. We have a little breakfast together sometimes, but he can be very cranky at that time of the morning. I always have to judge whether it's safe to talk to him or not. I rise quite early, you see. I always have. When I was a boy, I used to go running early every morning. I can't do that now, of course. My legs wouldn't stand for it. No one to blame for that but myself, I suppose.'

'It's hardly your fault,' said Noah. 'You can't help getting older.'

'I can't now, that's true,' said the old man, nodding his head. 'But I didn't have to get older. That was a decision I made myself.'

'How could you have—?' began Noah, but it was the old man's turn to look out of the window now.

'The sun will be going down soon,' he said. 'I remember once I saw the sun go down over Watson's Bay in Sydney, and later that day I ran all the way to the tip of southern Spain to watch it come up again.'

'You must have been very tired,' said Noah in astonishment.

'Well, yes, I'm only human,' said the old man, smiling.

'I've only ever seen one sunrise,' Noah said quietly. 'At my own house, of course.'

'Ah, then you're an early riser too?'

'Not usually,' he admitted. 'Sometimes my dad says he's going to throw a bucket of water on me if I don't get up. It's strange – I always complain when it's time to go to bed, and then I complain even more when it's time to get up. It doesn't make much sense, does it?'

'That,' said the old man, tapping a finger on the wooden table, 'is one of the great paradoxes of life. Was your sunrise very memorable then?'

Noah swallowed and looked away. He waited a long time before answering, and when he did his voice came out very quiet.

'Yes,' he said. 'I don't think I'll ever forget it.'

Chapter Nineteen

Sunrise

In the weeks that followed Noah's visit to the fair, his mother continued to feel very ill, and one night, when his father came home from a drive to the city that they'd taken together, she wasn't even with him.

'Your mum will be back tomorrow,' said Noah's father, who seemed very tired and appeared to be thinking about the answers he was going to give to Noah's questions rather than simply telling him the truth.

'Tomorrow?' asked Noah in surprise. 'But why? Where will she stay tonight?'

'In the city,' said Dad. 'With some friends.'

'But she doesn't have any friends in the city,' said Noah, who had heard his mother say many times that she wished they knew more people there so they'd have a reason to go in on a Saturday for lunch.

'Well, not friends exactly,' said Noah's dad. 'Look, it's difficult to explain. The important thing

167

is, she'll be home tomorrow, and tonight it's just the two of us. We can play football if you like.'

Noah shook his head and went to his room. He didn't want to play football. He wanted to be told the truth.

The next day she still wasn't home. It was the morning of the day when Noah had planned on starting to read his fifteenth book. He took it down off the shelf and opened it to the first page but couldn't concentrate on what was happening. There was somebody called Squire Trelawney and another man called Dr Livesey and an inn called the Admiral Benbow, and they all started to melt into one, not because it wasn't a good book but because Noah was finding it impossible to concentrate. He put it to one side and went downstairs to ask his father why his mum wasn't home yet.

'You said she'd be back today,' he said, and his father looked at him, and opened and closed his mouth for a few moments like a guppy fish.

'I said she'd be back tomorrow,' said his father.

'Yes, but that was yesterday. So today is tomorrow.'

'Now you're just being silly, Noah,' said Dad. 'How could today be tomorrow?'

Noah felt a great rage build up inside him. He had never felt anything like this before. It was like a hurricane of anger, starting in the pit of his stomach, twisting and turning, collecting bits of fury and pieces of temper as it whirled around, swept up through the centre of his body and finally came storming out of his mouth in a rush of indignation.

'I'm eight!' he cried, bursting into unexpected tears. 'I'm not five or six or seven any more. I want to know what's going on!'

But he didn't wait for a response, charging up to his room instead, locking the door behind him and throwing himself on the bed, refusing to open the door a few minutes later when his father knocked and said he wasn't to worry, his mother would be home soon. In fact he didn't even go down for his dinner that night, listening through his bedroom door when he heard his father talking on the phone later.

'All right, I'll wait,' he was saying to whoever was on the other end of the line. 'Hopefully he'll get some sleep and we can talk to him tomorrow.'

Noah was sure he wouldn't get any sleep that night, but as it turned out he was so exhausted by the time he got into bed, his head had barely touched the pillow when his eyes immediately closed and he drifted off into a dark dream from which he was very happy to wake when a hand shook his shoulder some hours later.

The room was still dark so he knew it wasn't morning yet, but he could sense a person sitting on the bed next to him, breathing very quietly, and he jumped up, frightened, and turned on the bedside light.

'Mum!' he cried, finding it hard to open his eyes as they adjusted to the sudden brightness. 'You're back.'

'I said I'd be back, didn't I?' she asked quietly. 'I shouldn't really be here but I couldn't stay away any longer. From you, I mean. I don't know what your father will say when he wakes up and finds that I . . . that I came home.'

'I missed you,' said Noah, throwing his arms around her, and despite how pleased he was to see his mother again, he was still very tired and would have liked to have gone straight back to sleep and talk to her in the morning when he was up and dressed. 'What time is it anyway?'

'It's still the middle of the night,' she replied, leaning over and kissing him on the top of his head. 'I wanted to show you something, that's all.'

Noah glanced across at his bedside clock and pulled a face.

'I know, I know,' said his mum before he could say anything else. 'But trust me, it'll be worth it.'

'Can't we do it later?' he asked.

'No, it has to be now,' she insisted. 'Come on, Noah. Please. Just get up. I promise you won't regret it.'

Noah nodded and climbed out of bed, and the two of them went downstairs and out of the front door and over to the far corner of their garden, where they could see right through the trees of the forest towards the horizon ahead. The grass felt damp under Noah's feet but he quite liked the sensation, and he twisted and turned his toes in the soil to let it spread around every one of them.

'Now watch,' said his mum, holding his hand, and he stared into the dark distance now, unsure what he was supposed to be watching out for. He swallowed and yawned, and then yawned once more, wondering when he could go back to bed. He heard a rustling in the grass to his right, and a dark brown fox with a striking white stripe along his back appeared for a moment, glanced at him, held his gaze for the longest time, and then disappeared into the tall grass that separated their house from the forest.

'What else am I supposed to be watching out for?' asked Noah, turning to his mother, and she shook her head and pointed into the distance again as she glanced at her watch.

'Just watch,' she said, holding his hand even tighter now. 'Any minute now.'

He narrowed his eyes, wondering what was going to happen.

'Here it comes,' said his mother after a moment. 'Now don't take your eyes off the horizon. Keep watching, Noah. It'll knock your socks off.'

'But I'm not wearing any socks,' said Noah, looking down at his bare feet, wet and green beneath him.

And then, a minute later, the most extraordinary thing happened. The darkness that covered the forest floor was suddenly illuminated by a bright sheet of golden sunlight which flooded through the dew-soaked leaves of grass and the branches of the trees, turning the whole world from night to day in a few short moments.

'You haven't lived until you've seen the dawn break over the forest,' said his mum, pulling him close to her. 'My dad brought me out to see it just before . . . just before he left us. And I never forgot it. It's one of my happiest memories of him. So I wanted us to see it together, just you and I, Noah. What did you think? Wasn't it wonderful?'

'It was nice,' he said with a shrug. 'Do I have to stay out here?' he asked after a moment. 'I'm freezing.'

Noah's mum looked at him a little sadly and shook her head. 'No,' she said. 'No, you can go back in if you want. I just wanted us to see it together once, that's all. Now, any time in the future you ever see the dawn break, maybe you'll think of me.'

Noah nodded and ran back to the house, charged upstairs and threw his dressing gown on the floor. Just before he got back into bed, however, he took a quick look out of the window and was surprised to see that his mother was still out there where he'd left her, about halfway along the fence, but she'd climbed the two wooden rungs like a ladder and was standing a few feet off the ground, the only person he could see in the great expanse of forest ahead – the only person awake in the whole world, he thought – her arms stretched out wide into the bright sunny morning, her head thrown back to receive the warmth of the sun on her face. It was an extraordinary sight.

A moment later he got back into bed, but despite how tired he was, he couldn't get back to sleep. Only when he heard his mother returning through the front door and walking slowly upstairs did he feel safe.

And that's when he heard her cry out, a great loud cry of pain, and he sat up in bed, not wanting to move, as he heard the door of his parents' bedroom open and his father go rushing down the stairs, calling her name.

Chapter Twenty

Noah and the Old Man

'I think I'm starting to understand,' said the old man. 'It can be a very lonely life, leaving all the people you love behind. You need to be very sure about what you're doing. The point comes, after all, where it's too late to go home.'

'But you came home,' said Noah. 'You kept your promise. Once you received the letter saying your father was ill. You came home again.'

'It's not quite as simple as that,' said the old man sadly, reaching for another piece of wood and staring at it for a long time before beginning to carve a pair of legs in the base of it. 'I haven't finished my story yet, after all. But look at the time,' he added. 'Don't you think it might be an idea not to run away after all? You could still get back home before dark if you wanted to.'

'I think I'd be in far too much trouble to return home now,' said Noah, looking a little regretful of his actions. 'I'd better stick with my original plan.'

'I'm sure your parents would forgive you,' said

the old man. 'They'd just be glad to have you back.'

Noah thought about it. Even though he'd only been gone from home for a few hours, he was already starting to miss it a little. But every time he thought of it, he also thought about the fact that to go back there was to face up to what was going to come next, and he wasn't sure if he was ready for that.

'But why not?' asked the old man, surprising Noah, for he was sure he hadn't spoken out loud. 'What comes next?'

'Bad things,' he replied.

'What kind of bad things?'

'Did you really never have a mother?' Noah asked the old man.

'No,' he replied sadly. 'Just a father. I often wished I had a mother, of course. I always thought they seemed like very nice people, most of them. Until today, that is.'

'Why?' asked Noah. 'What's so different about today?'

'Well,' said the old man with a laugh, 'you're telling me all these wonderful stories about your mother, about how kind she was to you, how thoughtful, but still you've run away from her. I can only assume that she's not as nice as you make her out to be.'

'But that's not it,' cried Noah in frustration, standing up and walking over to the window. 'Look,' he said after a moment, noticing a great to-do taking place outside on the street. 'There's a lot of people gathering outside.' He looked down to where a small crowd was standing, staring across at the toy shop and taking notes. The dachshund who had been so helpful to him earlier in the day was among their number, and he seemed to be growing quite energized as he discussed something with a red-faced, middle-aged man, who appeared to be in charge – for he was waving his arms in the air a lot and telling the people to keep quiet so he could think. The donkey was eating a banana that a woman had unpeeled but was still holding in the air as she stared across the road. 'What do they want?'

'Oh, I wouldn't mind them,' said the old man, refusing even to bother looking. 'Every so often they stand over there and write things down. Then they compose articles denouncing me to the village newsletter that everyone receives but no one ever reads. It's not that they have a problem with me. Or with this shop. It's really that tree they object to,' he said, pointing towards the branches, which were swaying a little in the late afternoon breeze and stopped the moment they realized they were being observed. 'They say it's not normal, what goes on here, but I say I don't care. Who asked for their opinion anyway? The dachshund will be on my side, not to worry. And the donkey. They'll keep the troublemakers at bay. Now, what do you think of this?'

Noah turned round and took the puppet the

Fig 11

WALL-mounted TIME-KEEPING DEVICE.

old man had just finished carving. It seemed to be some sort of mongoose. 'It's very good,' said Noah. 'How did you do it so quickly?'

'I have a lot of experience,' said the old man.

Noah watched the crowd again for a moment longer before sitting down on the window seat.

'Dad says that the doctors are going to make Mum better,' he said a few moments later. 'At least, that's what he used to say. Now he says that I have to be very brave.'

'And your mum?' asked the old man. 'Would I be right in thinking that she's in hospital?'

'She was,' said Noah, turning away so the old man wouldn't see the tears forming in his eyes. 'She's back home now. In bed. She came home yesterday, you see. She insisted on it. She said that was where she wanted to be when she – when she—' He found that he couldn't get the words out now, and scrunched up his face and hands to keep himself steady.

'But if she's at home and she's not well, shouldn't you be with her?'

Noah turned back and looked at the old man. 'You ran away from home too,' he said.

'But I came back,' said the old man, 'when I found out that my father was ill.'

'Did it take you long?' asked Noah, standing up now and helping him to clear the last of the cups and the glasses from the table. His stomach was full at last, and even though there was a tray of after-dinner chocolates standing on the counter next to him, he only glanced at them for a moment before shaking his head and looking away, leaving them to shuffle off despondently back to one of the cupboards. 'Did you get there in time, when you got the letter about your father being ill? Did you get home before he . . . before anything . . .'

'Before he died?' the old man said. 'What's the matter, boy? Can't you say the word? It's only a word, you know. Just a group of letters strung together in a random order. The word itself is as nothing compared to the meaning.'

'Yes, that,' said Noah, looking down at the floor and clenching his jaw and fists so tightly he thought his fingers might go right through his palms and out the other side if he wasn't careful. He noticed there was one last puppet in the box, and he took it out and looked at it – it appeared to be the puppet of an elderly rabbit whose whiskers twitched when you pulled his string – before placing it next to all the others. 'Did you get home before he died?'

Chapter Twenty-One

Dr Wings' Puppet

When I reached the toy shop (said the old man), everything seemed to be exactly as it was when I left it. The walls were still lined with toys, the floor was still scattered with sawdust, and behind the counter a few pots of paint were left with their lids half off, a gloopy rainbow of colours forging trails down the sides. A few cobwebs hung off the cash register. 'Hello?' I whispered, looking around, expecting my father to appear out of the shadows at any moment. 'Poppa?'

But there was no answer and I bit my lip, wondering what I should do next. The hospital was only a few miles away – I could be there in seconds if I put my mind to it – but something told me that Poppa would never have gone to a hospital. He had built this toy shop himself, after all. He had created it from the ground up, not just the misshapen bricks and misplaced mortar that held the thing together, but all the contents too, every one of the toys that ran along the counters and stood on the shelves. He would never leave here; I was sure of that.

A creaking sound from behind the counter made me look up, and I saw that the door had placed itself in position and was standing slightly ajar.

'Henry,' I cried. 'Henry, my old friend! You're still here.'

The door stared at me with an accusatory expression, allowing none of the former warmth and friendship that had once been between us to reappear. Instead it simply stood there quietly, allowing me a view of the dimly lit staircase beyond. I walked towards it and looked up at the spiral of wooden steps above my head and began to climb. Sensing the urgency of the moment, Henry soon brushed past me and fitted himself into the wall, this time remaining firmly closed but allowing me to turn his handle. A light was on inside the living room and I stepped inside, the floorboards creaking beneath my feet as I entered.

Nothing had changed. The chairs were in their usual places before the fireplace, although they immediately turned their backs on me when they saw who had stepped inside. The plates and cups were arranged on the sideboard, but they turned their handles round, unwilling to be picked up. The coat stand was still in the corner, but it tiptoed away on its four legs and disappeared into what had once been my boyhood bedroom, closing the door behind it.

It made me terribly sad to see how disappointed all my father's things were in me.

'Oh my!' said an elderly rabbit, appearing out of my father's bedroom and jumping in surprise at the sight of this most unexpected visitor, before relaxing and breaking into a smile. 'You came! I can hardly believe it! I didn't recognize you for a moment. You're so much older.'

'Hello, Dr Wings,' I said, stepping forward and stroking the rabbit's ears. I had always been very fond of the doctor, who had attended many of my childhood illnesses. 'I got your letter and came as soon as I could.'

'Ah, I see,' said Dr Wings, looking away for a moment and biting his lip. 'I wasn't sure if it would even reach you. You've been gone for so long, after all.'

'Yes, I got sidetracked,' I told him, unable to look the rabbit in the eye, so ashamed was I of my selfish actions. I had tried to be a good son, but the truth was, events kept getting in the way.

'Sidetracked?' asked Dr Wings, frowning. 'For all these years? When your father was growing older and more infirm? How extraordinary!'

'I am sorry about it,' I replied, looking down at the floor. 'But I'm here now. How is he anyway? Is he any better? I want to stay and take care of him now, really I do.' I hesitated for a moment, the worst possible thought coming into my head.

'He's not . . . he hasn't . . .'

'Oh my,' said Dr Wings sadly, shaking his head as he chewed on a carrot stick. 'If only you'd got here an hour earlier.'

'I tried to come home!' I explained, an enormous weight of guilt beginning to spread throughout my body. 'How did he get so ill anyway? He was fine when I left. Getting older, of course, but he wasn't in poor health.'

Dr Wings narrowed his eyes and looked at me thoughtfully. 'How long do you think you've been gone?' he asked.

'A few months, I suppose,' I said, my cheeks growing red. 'I lose track of time so easily. When you're running all the time, you go through so many different time zones, you never quite know where you are. Or when you are.'

'My boy, that's the most ridiculous thing I've ever heard,' said the rabbit, staring at the green roots sprouting from the end of the carrot before popping it into his mouth and swallowing it in one go. 'The fact of the matter is, you've been gone for almost ten years.'

'No!' I cried, looking at my watch as if that might confirm things one way or the other.

'I assure you, it's quite true.'

'So I've missed ten birthdays?' I asked.

'You've missed ten of your *father's* birthdays,' pointed out the rabbit. 'And throughout all that time, you were all he ever talked about. He followed

183

your exploits in the newspapers every week.'

'I certainly never meant to be away for so long,' I said. 'After all, I promised Poppa I would be back after the Olympic Games.'

'But you never came home,' repeated Dr Wings.

'No,' I admitted. 'No, I never did. How did he get ill?'

Dr Wings smiled kindly at me and shook his head. 'My boy, he got old, that's all it is. Your father was a very elderly man. He'd worked hard all his life. Why, he was still working in the toy shop until a few weeks ago. Then he started to suffer some dizzy spells and I came to see about them but there was nothing I could do. A few days later he had a fall, and after that he took to his bed. I'm afraid we've been losing him ever since.'

I shook my head. 'It's not something I thought would ever happen,' I said.

'But we all grow old,' said the rabbit. 'You're growing older yourself. That's what happens. Boys become men. And men become old men. You knew that much, of course.'

I nodded. I knew one thing that never grew old: a puppet.

'If you'd only arrived an hour earlier,' said Dr Wings sadly, shaking his head.

'Just an hour? You mean—?'

'Yes. He died just before you got home. He's in there, in bed. You can go in and see him if you want.'

I exhaled and walked slowly towards the

bedroom door, hesitating for only a moment as I looked inside, nervous of what I might see when my eyes adjusted to the gloom. The curtains were closed and the room remained in an evening shade of half-darkness. On my father's bedside table, a small lamp was snoozing quietly, but it sensed my presence, looked across, and its bulb burst into immediate brightness, so surprised was it by what it saw.

In the bed, Poppa lay looking for all the world as if he was fast asleep. He was older than I remembered him, but he looked at peace and I was glad of that.

'It's me, Poppa,' I whispered, stepping forward. 'I came home.'

After Poppa was laid to rest, it didn't take long for me to decide that I would have to do something to honour his memory. I hung up my running shoes and decided that I would make a go of his business instead. After all, Poppa had devoted so many years to building up the toy shop, it would be a shame to simply let it go just because its creator was no longer among the living. I made peace with everything in the shop that had been disappointed with my failure to return for so many years and we vowed to begin anew together, friends again.

Fortunately for me I had learned so many things in school after our move to the village that I knew exactly what I was doing too.

I rose every morning at four o'clock and ran for five hours before opening the toy shop, just to keep fit. When there were no customers, which was always, I would make new toys; all sorts of toys – trains and cars, footballs and boats, letter puzzles and alphabet blocks, but never puppets, never ever puppets – and then paint them, decide upon a price and place them on the appropriate shelf. When Alexander struck six o'clock in the evening, I would jump into my running clothes once again and set off for some of the more distant villages for a few hours before returning to the shop, locking up for the evening and retiring upstairs to eat my dinner. A little pasta, perhaps. Or a garden salad. I was in bed every night by midnight and up again by four, seven days a week.

All in all it was a good life, I told myself. And every day I tried not to think about how much I regretted leaving Poppa alone when he needed me most.

Chapter Twenty-Two

Noah and the Old Man

'I'm sorry your father died,' said Noah, looking down at the floor. 'Do you still miss him?'

The old man nodded and looked around the room. 'I think of him when I come in here every morning,' he said. 'When I eat my breakfast, when I'm looking forward to the day ahead. And at night when I'm sitting by the fire, reading a book, I imagine he's there beside me, watching over me. I feel him close by, and I tell him that I'm sorry I wasn't there at the end.'

Noah said nothing for a long time. He could hear a lot of conversations taking place in his head, a lot of arguments, some of which he wanted to listen to and some of which he wanted to ignore altogether.

'Can we go back downstairs?' he asked, standing up and rubbing his arms. 'It feels a little cold up here and I should probably be leaving soon anyway.'

'Of course, my boy,' said the old man, walking

over towards Henry and opening him up. 'Please, follow me.'

They walked out onto the staircase, stepping back for a moment to allow the door to go downstairs first, and once he was comfortably settled into the wall below, they turned his handle and went through into the toy shop once again.

'Doesn't it ever get lonely living here all alone?' asked Noah, looking around with the curious sensation that some of the puppets were now in different places from where they had been before.

'Sometimes,' admitted the old man. 'But I'm an old man now and amn't looking for company.'

'How old are you exactly?'

The old man considered this and scratched his chin. 'To be honest, I've lost track,' he said. 'But I'm no spring chicken, I know that much for sure.'

'I'm surprised you decided to stay here,' said Noah. 'After your father died, I mean. You could have had so many adventures for the rest of your life. You could have travelled the world.'

'But every day has been an adventure,' replied the old man, smiling. 'It doesn't matter whether I'm here with my puppets or ten thousand miles away. Something interesting always happens, wherever you are. I'm not sure if that makes sense but—'

'It does,' said Noah. 'Don't you ever sell any of these puppets?' he asked.

'Oh no,' replied the old man. 'No, they're not for sale.'

'Not for sale?' asked Noah, laughing. 'But this is a shop, isn't it?'

'It's a place where things are made, certainly. And there's a front door, of course. Most days. And over there is a cash register, although I'm not sure if it works any more. Is it a shop? Perhaps it is. I don't know. Does it matter? It's my home.'

Noah considered this and turned round, looked at his surroundings and took a few steps along the aisles of the shop, staring at the puppets as if they might offer up their secrets, before finally selecting two from the shelves, both traditional puppets of men.

'Do they have names?' he asked, holding up his finds.

'Oh yes,' said the old man, a great smile crossing his face. 'The one in your left hand is based on my father, Poppa. It's quite a good likeness actually. And the one in your right hand . . . well, he was a neighbour of Poppa's before I was born, Master Cherry. Pull their strings and you might see something you like.'

Noah looked down and pulled the strings that extended beneath the feet of the two toys. Their arms and legs rose as he expected them to, but – great delight! – the hair lifted off their heads as well.

'They're wearing wigs!' he cried, laughing.

'They always did,' explained the old man. 'They got into a terrible fight once and nearly lost those wigs.'

'What was the fight over?'

'A misunderstanding, that's all.'

'Oh. And did they become friends again afterwards?'

'Great friends,' said the old man in a satisfied tone. 'And they swore to remain so for the rest of their lives.'

Noah nodded, pleased with the story, and replaced the puppets on the shelves. 'And these,' he said, selecting two more and holding them out before him. 'The fox and the cat.'

'Terrible creatures,' said the old man, shaking his head and frowning, his voice growing deeper as he looked at the malevolent animals. 'Infamous villains, the pair of them. They robbed me of five gold coins and caused me to be sent to jail. Never trust a fox or a cat. There. I've said it.'

Noah's eyebrows danced up and down and he looked back at the shelves for another puppet.

'This one?' he asked, pointing at a brightly coloured creature.

'Ah, the cricket,' said the old man in delight. 'A fine fellow whom I mistreated badly.'

'Really?' asked Noah. 'What did you do to him?'

'I smashed him against the wall with a wooden hammer and killed him.'

Noah's mouth opened wide in horror. 'Why?' he asked. 'Why would you do such a thing?'

'He accused me of having a wooden head. I may have' – the old man glanced around and looked a little ashamed of himself – 'I may have over-reacted slightly. But don't look so aghast, boy,' he added. 'The cricket came back in a different form. A sort of ghost. We became firm friends after that.'

Noah shook his head but said nothing, merely pointed at the next puppet along the wall.

'Now that's a fellow I called the Fire-Eater. Not a nice man at all. Tried to burn me alive once. And beside him are two assassins who tried to murder me.'

'What's that in their hands?' asked Noah, leaning forward to take a closer look.

'A knife and a noose. They were torn between stabbing me and hanging me.'

'You certainly had your share of enemies when you were young,' said Noah in amazement.

'I did,' said the old man. 'I don't know why. People just seemed to take against me for some reason.'

'And you carved all these puppets yourself?'

'Every one.'

'How extraordinary!'

'They stay the same for ever,' said the old man, smiling a little. 'A puppet can travel and have adventures and never age a day. A boy . . . a real boy . . . he grows old and nothing lies ahead of him but death.' He stopped talking for a moment. When he looked up again, the boy was staring at him, his face filled with concern. 'You should never want to be anything other than you are,' the old man said quietly. 'Remember that. You should never wish for more than you have been given. It could be the greatest mistake of your life.'

Noah wasn't entirely sure what the words meant, but he stored them at the back of his mind, just above his right ear, certain that a part of him might want to dig them out again one day and have a think about them, and when that day came, he wanted them to be near at hand.

'Can I tell you a secret?' Noah asked.

'Of course you can,' replied the old man.

'And you won't tell anyone?'

The old man hesitated. 'Not a soul,' he said.

Noah's eyes opened wide. What was this? Could it possibly be? Was the old man's nose . . . *growing longer?*

'One person! One person!' cried the old man quickly, pressing the flat of his hand to the tip of his nose in embarrassment. 'I might tell one person, but only one.' At these words, his nose seemed to retract back to its regular position, and Noah blinked several times, unsure whether he had really seen what he thought he had seen or whether it had been an illusion of some sort. 'I have a friend,' explained the old man, smiling a little. 'A rather elderly pig who lives on a farm near here whom I visit regularly, and we share our secrets with each other. Would you mind if I told the pig? He's very discreet.'

Noah considered this for a few moments and finally nodded. 'I think that would be fine,' he said. 'But *just* the pig.'

'Just the pig,' agreed the old man.

'All right then,' said Noah. 'It's just that I think I might have made a mistake. Running away, I mean. I don't think I really thought about what it would mean.' He sighed and looked around, shaking his head suddenly as if he was trying to throw all these thoughts away, and staring at the puppets again instead. 'I think I should go home now. Can I have one, do you think?' he asked. 'To take with me?'

The old man considered this request for a long time but finally shook his head. 'I don't think so,' he said. 'I'm sorry, but they're a part of a family, you see. They remind me of my life.'

'But you could carve another, surely?'

'Oh no,' he said, shaking his head. 'It's a curious thing. Whenever I have a block of wood in front of me, whenever I sit down to create a puppet, I'm always trying to carve something else but for some reason it never turns out the way I intended. I start with one idea in mind, but then something entirely different appears out of the wood. Look at this, for example,' he said, holding up the piece of wood, which had been transformed into a baboon. 'I wasn't trying to make a baboon.'

'Then what were you trying to make?'

The old man looked away for a moment and shrugged his shoulders; it was time for him to tell the truth. 'Why, me, of course,' he replied with a smile.

Chapter Twenty-Three

The Master Craftsman

The truth was (said the old man), for many years I had avoided carving puppets. Instead I made trains and boats and letter blocks and pencil holders, and anything else I could think of that could be put together with wood and nails. I kept up the traditions that had begun with Poppa, and in some cases I even managed to improve on them.

And even though I was no longer travelling the world and having great adventures, I kept up my usual routines after his death, running in the mornings and evenings, although usually only doing a few thousand circuits of the village because I knew for certain that if I went any further, then I would only end up in some palace or festival, up the Pyramids or down the Grand Canyon, and I had a business to look after now and I had to put that first.

But then the strangest thing happened. One day, just as I was about to set off on my evening run, I noticed that I was feeling a little tired. I was reaching down to tie my laces, and when I stood up again

I let out an unexpected sigh of exhaustion and my hand moved quickly to the lower portion of my back, which was feeling terribly sore. And even though I went out that night, I came back panting a little more than usual and didn't even eat my supper before falling into bed. I didn't think too much about it until a few months later, when I found myself starting to groan every morning when Alexander's alarm went off and wanting to curl back up under the sheets and not do any running at all.

And as year followed year I realized that I had to cut back on my exercise. My body had become a little less supple, my legs a little less quick to respond to my demands. I was not as quick on my feet as I had once been. Small blue veins in my hands began to grow more pronounced. Once, I even came down with a cold.

And then, one day, while I was tidying one of the displays in the toy shop, I noticed my father, Poppa, standing only three feet away from me, looking as old as he was on the day I had gone to my triumphant Olympic Games all those years before. 'Poppa!' I cried, overjoyed to see him again, forgetting for a moment that he had died many years earlier. I ran forward, arms outstretched, just as Poppa ran towards me too, his arms also out-stretched.

We collided. I fell over. So did Poppa.

I looked up and realized that this was not my father at all; what I had seen was my own reflection in the long, wood-framed mirror that had stood for so many years in the corner of the shop.

I'm an old man now, I thought.

It was at that moment that I realized I had made the wrong decision all those years before when I had been granted my wish to become a real boy. I should have stayed a puppet.

As that idea settled in my head, I felt a curious sensation dissolving into my arms and hands, a feeling that could only be satisfied by taking a hammer and chisel in either fist and sitting down to work. I went downstairs to the basement, where I always kept a big supply of wood, and to my surprise, for the first time in my life, I discovered that I had none left. Of course, I normally purchased all my materials for the toys from a local lumberyard, but it was almost midnight and the yard would be closed until the following morning. But I had to carve a puppet; I had no choice. I wouldn't be able to sleep if I didn't. I wouldn't be able to *breathe.*

I stepped outside the toy shop and looked up and down the empty streets, allowing the night air to pour into my lungs, and wondered for a moment whether anyone would notice if I simply climbed over the wall into the lumberyard and stole enough for my needs. Well, not *stole* it as such, as I would certainly return the next day and pay for whatever I had taken, but as soon as the idea entered my head I realized that such a thing was impossible. My legs, after all, were not the legs they had once been.

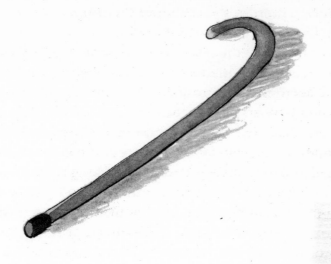

Fig 12

A WALKING STICK.
No longer used.

I couldn't jump the wall or even climb over it any more. (Even as a young man I'd only been able to manage silver in the 400-metre hurdles so it was entirely out of the question now that I was old.) The whole thing seemed impossible.

Filled with frustration, I turned my attention to the tree that stood before me and a thick branch caught my eye. Could it be that simple? It was almost as if the branch was calling out to me. *Take me!* it was saying. Come on, *snap me off!*

And so I did.

I took a firm hold of the branch and, surprising myself with a sudden discovery of strength, I wrenched it away from the trunk and stood rooted to the path as I stared at the clean, solid lump of wood that I held in his hands. A moment later, I stepped back inside the shop, locked the door behind me, went downstairs to the basement and got to work.

I knew exactly the puppet I wanted to create. I could see in my mind the straight, neat legs, jointed at the knees, the second set of feet that Poppa had created after I'd been foolish enough to allow the first set to be burned off while I slept. The smooth cylindrical body was easy to recall, as were the skinny arms and simple hands that stretched out from them. The cheerful, eager face; the trouble-some nose that grew and grew whenever I told a lie. It was all there; it was all locked away in my memory. I was sure I could do it; after all, I was a master

craftsman and had never attempted a carving that I had failed to produce.

'If I do this right . . .' I told myself as I chipped and chiselled away. 'If I make him perfect, then maybe, just maybe . . .'

And for a long time it looked as if it might just work. The legs *seemed* to be the right legs; the body *seemed* to be the right body; the face *seemed* to be the right face. But when I finished that first puppet and stepped away from it, I was astonished by what I saw. For it had mysteriously transformed into a fox – a fox I knew well, a fox who had persuaded me many years before to bury my five gold coins in the field of miracles, to water them and go away for a few hours so that when I returned they would have turned into five thousand gold coins. The fox who had stolen from me because of my innocence.

'Now, how did that happen?' I asked myself, shaking my head in surprise and determining that the next night I would concentrate more carefully on my work and then I would surely produce the perfect puppet.

From that evening on, night after night, I set about trying to create a wooden version of my former self, but every time I finished and looked at what I had produced, the puppet had become something entirely different. A puppet of a station master, perhaps. Or a grieving widow. A woman sitting at a desk composing a sonnet to a lover lost at sea. A feather floating in the breeze. A piano in need of tuning. The statue of Zeus at Olympia. Charles Lindbergh, setting off in the *Spirit of St Louis*. It didn't matter how the puppet began or how intensely I worked at my creation, it always turned into something entirely different and completely unexpected.

And every night I broke another branch off the tree and began again. And a few mornings after that, the branch had grown back.

This has been going on for years now. I have decorated the shop with the puppets that my hands have carved out of Poppa's tree, and all the time I've been growing older and older until finally I realize that my quest was hopeless.

I made my choice. I became a real boy and I can never be a puppet again.

And as Dr Wings pointed out, a real boy became a real man, and a real man became a real old man, and after that—

Chapter Twenty-Four

Noah and the Old Man

'I know what comes after that,' said Noah, looking
away, feeling his heart start to beat a little faster
inside his chest.

'Yes, I expect you do,' said the old man, sitting
down and smiling at the boy, his kindly eyes making
Noah feel warm and safe. 'Don't you think it's time
to go home now? To be with your mother while you
still can?'

Noah stood up. He was feeling tired and
confused. It had been a day filled with surprises and
adventures and all sorts of unexpected people and
incidents, and the truth was, he wanted nothing
more than to tell someone about all the things that
had happened to him. To tell someone he loved.

'I wish I could run a toy shop,' he said after a
few minutes, looking up with an excited expression
on his face. 'I think it must be wonderful to work in
a place like this.'

'I thought you wanted to be an astronomer,'
said the old man.

'That was just one of the professions I'm considering,' said Noah, correcting him. 'It might not be the right one for me. The thing is, I like toys very much. And I'm very good at woodwork. So perhaps I could have a job like yours some day?'

'It's possible,' said the old man, turning round to glance at Alexander the clock. 'My, is that the time already?' he said. 'It's getting late. It'll be dinner time soon.'

'But we've only just had lunch,' said Noah, knowing that he couldn't possibly eat another thing so soon or he would, quite simply, explode.

'And the sun is going down,' said the old man, looking out of the window at the sky, which was deepening into a dark blue with a few black clouds lingering on the horizon. 'I suppose I shall have to go for my exercise soon.'

'Do you still go running then?' asked Noah in surprise, for looking at the old man it was hard to imagine that he could possibly pick up any kind of speed; he was a little hunched over, for one thing, and even going up and down the staircase he had moved at a very slow pace.

'Oh no,' said the old man, shaking his head. 'No, I couldn't manage that any more. But I like to go for a walk every evening. Just around the village, that's all. To get a little fresh air in my lungs and to keep the blood circulating. Perhaps you'd like to join me this evening?'

Noah looked at his watch. He hadn't thought

very much further than leaving home and finding a village he liked, but now that he had found one, he didn't know what he was supposed to do next. 'Yes, all right,' he said, taking his jacket from the coat stand that came running towards him at just the right moment. 'I suppose a walk would be good for me too after all that food, but then I really need to be getting along.'

'Of course,' said the old man, taking his own coat and scarf off the stand too. 'Thank you, William,' he said to the stand, who tipped his head where the hats rested and ran back to the corner of the toy shop. 'A boy who has left home must keep on the move. He can never stop anywhere in case he's found. Why, he might run the risk of making friends if he stayed in the same place for too long.'

'I'm sure I could stop *somewhere*,' said Noah quickly. 'They'll give up looking for me eventually.'

'Oh, my dear boy,' replied the old man, laughing a little. 'If you think that, then you don't know your parents at all. They'll never stop looking for you. They'll always want you back. Now, do you have everything you came with?'

Noah took one last look around the shop and nodded. He didn't really want to go but knew that he couldn't stay there alone either. The toy shop was a strange and confusing place but he felt safe inside it.

'Good,' said the old man. 'Then we'll be on our way.'

They stepped out into the evening air, which was a little brisk. The street was quiet though, and there was no sign of the helpful dachshund, the hungry donkey or the crowd that had gathered outside earlier.

'Aren't you going to lock the door,' asked Noah, 'in case someone breaks in?'

'The simplest way to prevent a break-in is to leave the door unlocked,' explained the old man, turning to his right. 'It's the most obvious thing in the world but no one ever thinks of it. Now, come along, let's go this way.'

They walked past Poppa's tree and Noah looked at it once more. It did seem like a perfectly normal sort of tree really, although there was no question that the wood gave off a greater shine and lustre than the trees that were in the forest near his own house.

'I wish I could try carving something from the wood of that tree,' said Noah.

'Oh, that wouldn't be possible, I'm afraid,' said the old man, shaking his head. 'That tree is strictly the property of the toy shop. And you can't really sit down to carve toys or puppets unless you have practised it for many years and learned your trade,' he continued. 'You have to work very hard at it. And you need access to a lot of good wood too.'

'How extraordinary!' said Noah, breaking into a smile. 'Because my father is a lumberjack, and our house is situated on the edge of the forest, so I'd

204

have all the wood I needed. If I wanted to try it, I mean.'

'You also need good equipment,' continued the old man. 'A solid chisel, a strong plane, some sharp knives. And paint, of course. Quality paints.'

'Uncle Teddy!' cried Noah.

'Uncle who?'

'Uncle Teddy! He runs a paint store. He has over three thousand different varieties of paint. *If we don't 'ave it, it don't exist, mate* – that's his motto.'

'Also,' said the old man after a moment, considering the matter further, 'in order to run a business, you need to be good at sums. Otherwise you'll never balance the books.'

'I'm not very good at them,' admitted Noah. 'Although I was starting to get better. At school, I mean. My teacher said I had started to get the hang of them. Fractions and decimals anyway. I'm afraid I never really understood trigonometry.'

'Ah, well, trigonometry is about as useful to a boy as a bicycle is to a fish,' said the old man. 'So I wouldn't worry about that too much if I was you. It's important to be good at writing though,' he added. 'In order to write letters to your suppliers.'

Noah's head was fizzing with ideas and he looked at the ground, his fists bouncing on his knees as he considered his options.

'I wonder . . .' he began. 'If I *was* to go back . . . well, if I was to go back for just a little bit. I mean, until I was a year or two older, that's all. Until I was better at my sums, for example.'

'And your writing,' said the old man.

'And my writing,' said Noah. 'Then maybe I could become as skilful a craftsman as you. And I could open my own toy shop someday!'

'It's possible,' said the old man, stopping at a crossroads and breathing heavily. 'Stranger things have happened. I, for example, once saw a caterpillar debating with a whale. And winning the argument too. Do you mind if we stop here for a moment?' he asked then. 'I'm feeling a little tired.'

'Of course,' said Noah, looking around and spotting a bench only a few feet away. 'Why don't we sit over there?'

The old man nodded and they walked towards it and sat down. 'That's better,' he said with a sigh. 'It's a terrible thing growing old. The idea that I, the greatest runner in history, am unable to walk to the edge of my own village without having to stop and take a rest – well, it's something I never could have imagined happening to me.'

Noah turned to look at the old man and hesitated, wanting to phrase this question just right. 'Do you think . . . ?'

'I do sometimes, my boy,' admitted the old man. 'When I can't avoid it.'

'No,' said Noah, shaking his head. 'What I wanted to ask was, do you think I could stay here with you?'

'What, here?' asked the old man, looking around. 'On a bench at a crossroads? It doesn't seem like a very sensible plan.'

'Not *here*,' said Noah. 'I meant at the toy shop. I could come and live with you and you could train me up. I could learn all about woodwork and carving and I could keep the shop open if you ever fancied a holiday.'

'I have no plans to take any further holidays,' said the old man, smiling and patting the boy's hand. 'My travelling days are behind me, I'm afraid.'

'Well, I could run the shop at night. When you're asleep. It could be open twenty-four hours.'

'But I don't think we'd have the passing trade to support it,' said the old man, frowning. 'No, I don't think so, my boy. It doesn't seem like a very sensible idea.'

'Then maybe I could just be your apprentice,' suggested Noah. 'You could teach me all you know. I could be a great help to you and—'

'Noah,' said the old man in a kind voice, smiling at him, 'you forget that you already have a home of your own.'

'Do I?' asked the boy, wondering whether that was the case or not.

'Of course you do.'

'I'm not sure it will feel like home any more,' Noah said, narrowing his eyes and looking down the road ahead to where the path twisted and turned and led back towards the second village, and then the first, and then towards the forest and his own collection of stone walls, where his mother lay in bed.

'It may feel different,' said the old man. 'But that doesn't mean you shouldn't go back to it. I left my poor father alone for so long, and when I returned, well, it was too late for us. I wanted to see the world and was only interested in satisfying myself. I don't think you want to see the world, do you?'

'I do,' cried Noah enthusiastically. 'Well, some-day anyway,' he added in a quieter voice.

'And if you do, if you continue on your way, don't you think the day will come when you will be filled with as many regrets as I am?'

Noah nodded. The truth was, he was starting to long for his own home and his own bed. And even though he didn't yet know how his mother's story was going to end, she was still there now, she hadn't gone anywhere, and she had been right to want to spend as much time with him as possible while she still could. It was time for him to do the same thing. He didn't know how much longer they might have together, but even if it was just a day or two, that might still be enough time to build a lifetime of memories.

Noah tapped his left foot on the ground for a few moments, opened his mouth, closed it again, opened it, hesitated, and then came to a decision.

'I've decided to go home,' he announced, standing up.

'Very sensible,' said the old man.

'But do you think . . . ?' asked Noah, looking across at his new friend hopefully. 'Do you think that I could come back sometime? Just on a visit? And to watch you work? I'm sure I could learn a lot from you.'

'Of course,' said the old man. 'But you'll have to forgive me if I spend most of my time chipping away at old pieces of wood. I can't seem to help myself.'

Noah smiled and turned round, looking off in the direction from which he had come. It had grown dark now, but somehow he didn't feel frightened any more. He knew he wouldn't come to any harm.

'Would you like me to walk you back to the toy shop?' he asked. 'I can if you like.'

'No, no, my boy,' said the old man, shaking his head. 'It's a very kind offer but I think I'll stay here a little longer and just enjoy the evening air. My friend the donkey passes by here most evenings around now. I expect he'll be along soon and we can have a little chat before I go home again.'

'All right then,' said Noah, shaking hands with the old man. 'Thank you for today. For lunch, I mean. And for showing me around your toy shop.'

'You're very welcome,' said the old man.

'I'd better be going then,' said Noah, turning round; then, dashing off down the street in the darkness, running as fast as he could, he disappeared into the night.

Noah Barleywater arrived home late at night, after the sun had set, after the dogs were asleep, after the rest of the world had already gone to bed.

He ran down the laneway that led to his house, hearing nothing except the rubbing of the crickets and the hooting of the owls, and looked up at the only light that was turned on, in the upstairs bedroom of the cottage, where his parents slept. He stopped for a moment and stared at it, swallowing nervously, and wondered how much trouble he would be in for running away, but he didn't really care; the only thing that mattered was, he hadn't left it too late. Afraid now to go inside in case the worst had happened, he might have stood in the cold for hours had the front door not opened a moment later and his father looked out, discovering his son standing there, alone in the darkness.

'Noah,' he said, staring at him, and Noah bit his lip, unsure what to say.

'I'm sorry,' he whispered after a moment. 'I was afraid. So I ran away.'

'I was worried about you,' said Noah's father, not sounding angry at all, but relieved. 'I was going to look for you but something told me you were safe.'

'I'm not too late, am I?' asked Noah, asking the

question whose answer he feared the most. 'I still have time to—'

'You're not too late,' said his father, smiling a little. 'She's still with us.'

Noah breathed a sigh of relief and stepped inside, but as he did so, his father placed both his hands on the boy's shoulders and looked into his eyes. 'But, Noah, it won't be long now. You realize that, don't you? She doesn't have long left.'

'I know,' said Noah, nodding his head.

'Then let's go upstairs,' said his father, putting an arm around his shoulder. 'She'll want to see us now. Soon it will be time for her to say goodbye.'

They went upstairs together, and Noah stood in the doorway of his parents' bedroom looking at his mother.

'There you are,' she said, turning her face towards him and smiling. 'I knew you'd come home to me.'

Chapter Twenty-Five

The Final Puppet

The old man sat on the bench for a little while longer, thinking about the events of the day, and it was only when his friends, the dachshund and the donkey, passed by that he found himself ready to make his way back to the toy shop.

'The boy went home then?' asked the dachshund, looking around to check that they were alone. 'I thought he would in the end.'

'Yes,' said the old man, raising a hand to greet the cuckoo clock, who was hovering overhead now, letting him know that another hour had passed.

'I've never really trusted people who live at the edge of the forest,' remarked the donkey. 'They seems like a very unsavoury lot. I've gone there myself a few times, just to see what it was like, and I've noticed that they do the most extraordinary things. Do you know, I once saw a young woman holding a Labrador on a lead as they walked along together, as if she owned him or something.'

'Yes, they have some strange ways,' agreed the

old man. 'But they're not all bad. Remember, I used to live there myself. Poppa and I had a little cottage, and from my bedroom window I could see the forest opening up in front of me. They weren't bad days really.'

'Yes, but you came to live in the village,' said the dachshund. 'You had sense.'

'That was more my father's decision than mine,' replied the old man. 'Although I am glad he brought us here.'

'Hee-haw! Hee-haw!' cried the donkey, growing very agitated at this.

'Oh no,' said the old man, shaking his head. 'No, I can't agree with you on that. Things would have been different, certainly. But I wouldn't have wanted to live anywhere else. It's suited me, this life in the toy shop. I've been happy here.' He hesitated at the front door and looked up at the little mis-shapen building, put together with so much love by Poppa, and felt those old regrets returning to torment him.

'Do you think he'll come back someday?' asked the dachshund, turning round for a moment as he trotted off. 'The boy, I mean. Will he come back to visit?'

'It's possible,' said the old man with a smile. 'He found his way here once. Who's to say he won't find his way back again? Goodnight, my friends. I'm sure I'll see you all tomorrow.'

It was almost midnight by now, and after such

an exhausting day he felt quite tired, but then he had never enjoyed such prolonged company during a day and it had quite worn him out. Still, a night never went by when he didn't do a little carving before bed, and so he pulled a branch from Poppa's tree – it came away easily in his hands, as it always did – and closed the door behind him before making his way downstairs to the workshop. Sitting down, he took a chisel and hammer between his two ageing fists and started to work, stripping the bark away and smoothing down the lumber beneath his hands before beginning his latest figure.

It wasn't long before the wood started to take on the form of the puppet of a boy – but then it always did at this early stage. It was only later, as he came closer to the end, that it transformed itself into something else entirely.

Still the old man worked on.

But what a foolish puppet he had been, he decided, memories of his life passing through his mind as he chipped away at the wood. Choosing to exist as a boy and then as a man, over the wonderful adventures he might have had for all eternity; over the places he might have visited, the friends he might have made. Why had he ever thought that he would be better off as flesh and blood? It was almost too much to conceive of. A great weight of sadness descended upon him and he tried to quell these emotions as he continued with his work.

How extraordinary! he thought as he came closer to the end. *It looks so familiar. But any minute now it will change, surely?*

He laid down his chisel and his knives and held the puppet up to his eyes. A small boy with straight, neat legs, jointed at the knees, a smooth cylindrical body, and a pair of skinny arms and simple hands that stretched out from them. A cheerful, eager face. A troublesome nose. And now, a radiant smile. He had succeeded at last.

'Pinocchio,' he said.

Fig 13.

~~Pinnoch~~

PINOCCHIO'S
PUPPET.

Chapter Twenty-Six

Ten Years Later

The letter arrived on the morning of Noah's eighteenth birthday. He was lying in bed remembering
how he always used to wake up very early on this day
when he was a child, and run downstairs to see what
presents might be waiting for him, but he decided
not to do this year. He was a man now, after
all, and it would be a bit silly to rush downstairs
too quickly. He smiled when he remembered the
way his mother always used to make him a special
birthday breakfast, but this was one of those
recollections that didn't make him feel sad any
more; if anything, it made the smile on his face
grow even wider as he recalled those happy memories from the first eight years of his life that had
helped to shape him into the person he'd become.

He was really very lucky, he decided. Some
people had no happy memories at all; he had eight
years with his mother and eighteen with his father.
Not bad, all things considered.

He climbed out of bed and stepped across to

the desk that stood on the other side of the room. *That's a surprise,* he thought, seeing his chisel sitting on the corner of the desk, for he was sure he had left it downstairs in his workshop the night before. *Did Dad bring it up here in the night?*

A tap on the door made him turn round, and a moment later his father came in to wish him a happy birthday. There were presents from Auntie Joan, Cousin Mark, Uncle Teddy, and a rather surprising envelope too.

'Who's this from?' asked Noah, holding it in his hands and staring at it as if it was a time bomb that might go off at any moment.

'I don't know,' said his father. 'It arrived by special delivery first thing. You'll have to open it to find out.'

Noah slipped his finger under the seal and lifted out a long document, which he scanned quickly before opening his eyes wide and going back to read it carefully from the start.

'What is it?' asked his father, and Noah simply shook his head and handed it across.

'I think you'll need to read this for yourself,' he said.

The following day, Noah Barleywater collected the keys to Pinocchio's Toy Shop and made his way towards the village. His father had wanted to accompany him but he said no, not today, he wanted to go there on his own. It had been ten long

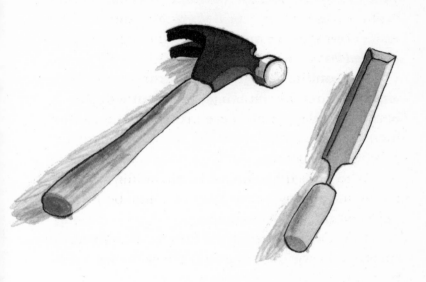

FIG 14

Tools REQUIRED for
CARPENTRY

years since he had last been inside, and it astonished him to remember that day when he was a child and had arrived in the village to meet the master craftsman, and the number of strange occurrences that had taken place. He had promised to come back and visit the old man again, but somehow, once he got home, the memory of that day had seemed to dissolve in his mind until it almost disappeared. In fact, he almost never thought of it again in all the years in between, not even when he told his father that he wanted to learn more about woodwork and carving, and had organized an area of the basement where he taught himself all the rudimentary secrets of planing and shaving, chipping and cutting, painting and designing – all the things that went into making toys of his own. He'd become very good at it too, and sold them at spring festivals and the various market days around the town.

In fact, it wasn't until the letter arrived on the morning of his eighteenth birthday telling him he would inherit the entire place, lock, stock and barrel, that all those memories came flooding back. There was one proviso on the inheritance though: that he reopen the shop and continue to trade in wooden toys and puppets. No plastic, no metal, just wood.

'Well, I can do that,' he said, thrilled by this unexpected gift, for it had been his intention to make a career as a toymaker anyway, and here was the perfect place to get started.

The shop was locked when he arrived, and he put the key in the door, opening it slowly, thinking that he had better oil the creak. He glanced up, and the bell gave a deep sigh and then an exaggerated ring, and he smiled at it, thinking he was going to have to have a word with it about its attitude. He wasn't surprised to find that, inside, the floor and counter tops were covered in dust.

Well, nothing that a good spring clean won't fix, he thought to himself, and set about taking all the old toys and puppets off the shelves and storing them neatly in the back room while he began the process of restoring the shop to its former glory and beginning his new life as a master toymaker.

He spent the rest of his days there, of course, happy and cheerful, working with wood and chisel and plane. A life filled with joy, as all lives should be. And unlike his predecessor, he never made a toy that didn't sell, for, quite soon, Pinocchio's Toy Shop – he kept the name – became one of the most successful businesses in a fifty-three-mile radius. Indeed, the only puppets that were never taken off the shelves over the years were that curious cast of characters that the old man's poppa, Geppetto, had carved and who he had introduced him to on the day they had first met: Mrs Shields, Mr Wickle, the Prince, Mr Quaker, Dr Wings . . . all of them went undisturbed. No customer ever picked them up. No visitor ever even glanced in their direction. It was almost as if they didn't see them at all. But Noah kept them there as a memento, because they belonged to a day he didn't want to forget ever again.

In fact, everything the old man had left behind was still present in the shop on the morning that Noah arrived, and he cared for and looked after every piece as if it was made of gold. Except for *one* thing, that is, which Noah didn't even notice when he first stepped inside.

A single wooden puppet that had sat on the counter gathering dust throughout those ten long years before the inheritance became his.

A puppet of a boy, with straight, neat legs, jointed at the knees, and a smooth cylindrical body.

It was sitting there when Noah first entered the shop. He left the door wide open as he surveyed his new home, allowing anyone to step inside, or run out.

And when he turned round again –
As if by magic –
Pinocchio's puppet –
Had disappeared.

Acknowledgements

Many thanks to David Fickling, Bella Pearson, Simon Trewin, Jane Willis, and the teams at Random House Children's Books and United Agents for all their advice and encouragement. And to Con, for constant love and support.

John Boyne

John Boyne was born in Ireland in 1971.
He is the author of seven previous novels
including the international bestsellers *Mutiny on
the Bounty, The House of Special Purpose* and *The
Boy in the Striped Pyjamas,* which won two Irish
Book Awards, topped the *New York Times*
Bestseller List and was turned into a Miramax
feature film. His books are published in over
forty languages. He lives and writes in Dublin.

www.johnboyne.com